Alba Arango

THE MYSTERIOUS MUSIC BOX

A DECODERS MYSTERY

Library of Congress Control Number: 2018911907

ISBN: 978-1-7327321-1-7 (Paperback)

To Mamy and Papy
Thank you for everything you have done for me.

CONTENTS

1 A NEW MYSTERY

At just before three in the afternoon, Steve walked up to the doors of the popular diner, Tyrone's, smoothed back his slight afro, and inhaled a deep breath. In a few minutes, the Decoders' new client, their first *real* client, would meet them here, inside these doors.

A couple months ago, Steve and his two best friends, Matt and Jenny, had formed a secret detective group called the Decoders. So far, all three cases they had solved involved helping someone they knew. Today, that would change.

Exhaling slowly, he entered Tyrone's. The smell, a cross between fried chicken and grilled hamburgers, immediately calmed his nerves. The three friends ate there so often, the diner had become like a second home. He had even memorized the location of all the different sports memorabilia decorating the walls. He spotted Matt and Jenny sitting at a booth, talking to Tyrone Washington, the owner of the restaurant.

"Hey, Steve," the tall, dark man greeted as the boy slid into the seat next to Matt. "Heard you all got yourselves a new case already." The only adult in Beachdale who knew their secret, Tyrone had been a huge help to the detectives on their previous cases. Their last mystery, *The Sleepwalking Vampire*, involved helping Tyrone's family solve a robbery.

Nodding, Steve glanced at the front door. "Yes. Alysha said our client would meet us here at three."

"What's the new case about?" Tyrone asked.

Steve pulled one of the glasses of water sitting at the center of the table toward him. "We aren't a hundred percent sure, but it has something to do with a missing music box. A girl from our school read Alysha's articles about our cases in the local newspaper and contacted her about hiring the Decoders."

Jenny tied her long blonde hair in a ponytail. "Can you blame her? The way Alysha writes those articles makes us sound like the greatest detectives ever."

Grinning, Matt linked his hands behind his head and reclined back. "Dudes, we *are* pretty awesome."

Jenny rolled her eyes. "Well, some of us are."

Laughing, Tyrone pulled out an order form and a pen from his apron pocket. "So, what can I get my favorite twelve-year-olds to eat on this fine Tuesday afternoon?" Matt ordered a double cheeseburger with fries while Steve and Jenny each ordered a chocolate shake.

At three-twenty, the young girl finally walked through the front doors. With waist-long, jet black hair and dark brown eyes, she looked exactly as Alysha had described her. She glanced around, noticeably nervous. Steve waved her over.

After scanning the diner, she slowly made her way over to their booth.

Steve stood and gave a short wave. "Hi, Rosa. My name is Steve Kemp, and these are my colleagues Matt Peterson and Jenny Reed. We are the Decoders."

The girl's dark eyes widened. "You are the detectives?" She spoke with an accent, but not difficult to understand.

He nodded, motioned for her to sit next to Jenny at the booth, and then sat facing her. "We spoke to Alysha yesterday. She told us you're missing a music box, but we need to get more details if we are going to help you find it."

Just then, Tyrone walked up to remove their plates. "How was everything?"

"Amazing, as always." Steve gestured toward the newcomer. "Tyrone, we'd like you to meet Rosa

Romero. She's a student at our middle school and our new client."

The tall man shook Rosa's hand warmly. "It's a pleasure to meet you. And congratulations on picking the best detective team here in Beachdale, California. Can I get you anything to drink or eat?"

She shook her head. "No, thank you."

"All right then. You all take your time. Let me know if you need anything."

The kids thanked him and he left, heading toward the kitchen.

Fiddling with the silver ring on her right hand, Rosa seemed a little disappointed. "I'm sorry for my surprise. I didn't know you were kids. The stories I read in the newspaper, I thought..." Her voice trailed off.

"The stories are all true," Steve said. He understood her concern. "The three of us are the detectives who solved all those cases."

After pushing her empty shake glass forward, Jenny leaned back into the seat and nodded. "We just can't let the world know who we really are. If our parents like ever found out about us, they would ground us for life."

Rosa half-smiled, reached into her purse, and took out fifty dollars. "It isn't much, but it's all I have now. My father gets his paycheck in two days. I can give you more then." She offered the money to Steve.

He shook his head and gently pushed her hand away. "The Decoders do not work for money."

"That's right," Matt said. "We work to help people. And right now, you're the one that needs our help." He grinned and placed his elbows on the table, but one of them hit his water glass, spilling the contents all over the table. His face turned slightly red. "Oops." He grabbed a stack of napkins from the dispenser next to him and began cleaning up the water. In doing so, he knocked over another glass of water. As he attempted to pull out more napkins, he knocked the dispenser over as well.

Noticing the twinkle in Jenny's eye, Steve knew if he didn't intervene immediately, she would tease Matt mercilessly. He whipped out his cell. "In order for us to help you, we need to ask you a few questions." He opened the notebook app. "Alysha said you needed to find a music box that belonged to your grandfather. Does he live around here?"

The girl blinked several times as though fighting back tears. "No. He…he died two weeks ago."

Reaching over, Jenny placed a hand on her shoulder. "We're so sorry."

Rosa opened her purse and pulled out a tissue. "That is why I must find his box."

Jenny withdrew her hand. "What happened to it?"

"It was stolen."

Steve's eyebrows shot up in surprise. A stolen music box could be difficult to track down. According to a news program he saw a few days earlier, only thirteen percent of robberies were ever solved. But impossible odds had never stopped the Decoders before. He gritted his teeth and smiled. "Let's start at the beginning. Tell us about your grandfather."

Rosa fiddled with the ring on her finger again. It appeared to calm her nerves. "He moved here from Mexico around six months ago after his work closed down."

"What did he do for a living?" Jenny asked.

"He worked in a museum as a...*cómo se dice*...do...do..."

"Docent," Steve finished.

Rosa clapped once. "Yes. That's it. A docent."

Drying off the last of the spilled water, Matt made a giant pile of all the wet napkins. "What's a docent?"

Steve typed into his cell. "It's the person who gives tours at a museum."

"Well, that's a *docent* way to make a living." Matt burst out laughing.

Steve and Jenny groaned.

Rosa smiled.

"What kind of a museum did he work for?" Steve asked.

"A history museum. It had things from all over

the world. My favorite were World War II things smuggled out of Germany."

Just then, Tyrone walked up and pointed to the pile of wet napkins. "What's up with that?"

Matt shook his head. "Don't ask."

Scooping the wet pile onto his tray, the owner promised to return with more water.

"What did your grandfather do once he moved here?" Steve asked.

"He found work at the Beachdale Museum. He even had some of the things from his old job sent here." Sadness spread across her face. "But then he got sick. We moved him to a nursing home where they could take care of him." Her eyes swelled with tears and she blinked several times. "He died two weeks ago."

Jenny reached over and gave her a quick hug. "We're so sorry."

After wiping her face with the tissue, the girl continued. "The day before he died, I went to see him. He gave me a music box and said I must keep it safe for him. He said inside was the key to great fortune."

"What did the music box look like?" Steve asked.

Rosa took a cell phone out of the back pocket of her jeans and showed them a picture of it. The red jeweled box had gold threading on it.

"Can you text that to me?" Steve asked.

She nodded and Steve gave her his number.

Tyrone walked up and placed four water glasses and straws down on the table. He nudged Matt. "Think you can keep these upright?"

The brown-haired boy cringed. "Um, yeah."

After the owner left laughing, Matt cleared his throat and put a straw in his new glass. "What was inside the box, anyway?"

Rosa lowered her gaze and shrugged. "Nothing. It was empty. And when I told him that, he laughed and said again that inside was the key to great fortune."

Frowning, Jenny reached for a new straw. "But if it had nothing in it, then what did he mean?"

The Mexican girl sighed. "I don't know. My grandfather, when he got sick, it hurt his mind. Sometimes, he thought he was a young man again. Sometimes, he thought he was back in Mexico." Her eyes teared up. "I know he was not okay, but that box meant a lot to him. He asked me to keep it safe, and I failed."

As a tear rolled down her cheek, she pleaded, "You must help me find it."

Matt reached back to the booth behind them and brought over the napkin dispenser. He pulled one out and handed it to her. "We will."

Steve glanced up from his notes. "You said the box was stolen. What happened?"

Her eyes narrowed, a look of concentration

taking over her face. "My father and I left Friday night to visit my *tia* in San Diego. We got back Sunday, two days ago, and found the house a mess, furniture turned over, papers thrown everywhere. The crooks stole many things, and the music box."

"Jerks," Jenny said in a huff and crossed her arms. "Did you call the cops?"

Rosa nodded. "Right away. They said it had probably been a 'crime of opportunity.' They had us make a list of everything taken. We couldn't believe our bad luck. First my grandfather, then this." She paused, inhaled a deep breath, and then exhaled slowly. "But then God smiled on us. The police found our stuff."

Surprised, Steve looked up. "Wait. The police found everything already?"

The girl smiled. "Yes. They found our stolen things at a pawn shop yesterday. Only the music box is still missing." She blinked several times. "I have to get it back."

Staring down at the notes he had typed, Steve bit his lip. How could everything have been recovered so quickly? Something felt wrong. "At which pawn shop did they find your things?"

She thought for a moment. "The police said they were at a place called Pawn Brothers."

He made a note. "And at what nursing home did your grandfather stay at?" Realizing the sensitivity of the subject, he added, "I know we're asking a lot of questions, but it's important for us to know every possible detail. We may have to go see these places for ourselves."

"Sunrise Acres." Her face lit up. "Um, my father and I are going there tomorrow to pick up my grandfather's things. Would you like to come?"

If her grandfather had left behind any clues about the importance of that music box, this could be their only chance to find them. Steve nodded. "Yes. That'd be perfect."

Rosa's phone beeped and she checked the message. "It's my father. I must go. I'll text you later about tomorrow." She stood and said good-bye.

Jenny waited until Rosa had disappeared out the door. "OMG. Matt, you are so crushing big time."

Matt turned slightly red. "I am not."

Knowing the direction the conversation would go if he didn't intervene, Steve held his hand up. "Stop. We have a much bigger problem than Matt's obvious crush."

"It's not a crush," Matt mumbled.

Jenny frowned. "What do you mean? What bigger problem?"

Glancing around to make sure no one could hear him, Steve lowered his voice. "I don't believe the robbery was an accident. I think the thieves wanted the music box."

Matt's eyes widened. "How do you figure that?"

"Think about it. Rosa said that the house had been ransacked. That's not usually what burglars do. A typical thief takes what he sees and runs, unless he's searching for something specific."

"But the robbers took a bunch of stuff, not just Rosa's box," Matt said.

Steve nodded. "But if the music box had been the target, then it would make sense for the crooks to take other things to make it look like a regular robbery, or a 'crime of opportunity' as the police put it."

After pushing a stray blonde hair behind her ear, Jenny shook her head. "But I still don't get it. What makes you think they were specifically after the music box?"

"Because the crooks pawned everything else. Why not the music box?"

The girl shrugged. "Maybe one of the robbers liked it and wanted to keep it."

"Or," Steve said, "perhaps the thieves believed the same thing the grandfather did...that inside was the key to great fortune."

"But it had nothing in it," Matt said. "I mean, wouldn't whoever took it have checked inside and saw it was empty?"

Sighing, Steve closed his notebook app. "I don't know. But I do know one thing for sure, fortune or no fortune, our job is to track down that music box."

Jenny nodded. "Okay. Where should we start?"

"Good question." Steve did a search for Pawn Brothers on his cell. "I say we begin at the pawn shop. Perhaps the owner can tell us something about the people who sold him Rosa's things."

Swigging down one last gulp of water, Matt stood. "Don't you think the police already did that?"

Steve headed toward the front door. "Yeah, but somehow I don't believe the cops are going to share what they discovered with us. We have to find out the details for ourselves."

After retrieving their bicycles from the bike rack, the trio headed toward Pawn Brothers to begin their investigation. Once inside, they waited until the man behind the register had no line and then asked about Rosa's stuff and if the thieves had also pawned the music box

The cashier studied the detectives curiously. "What's it to you kids?"

Jenny smiled. "You see," she said sweetly, "Rosa Romero is a good friend of ours from school. We're just trying to help her out." Her eyes grew teary. "I just can't believe those evil men took her music box. Her grandfather gave it to her on his deathbed." She dabbed her eyes with the sleeve of her shirt.

One thing Steve could definitely say about Jenny, she sure knew how to put on an act.

The man seemed sympathetic. "Look, it's like I told the cops; it was just the one guy and I don't remember too much about him. It was Saturday morning, we were super busy. He was a white guy, kinda chubby, with reddish-brown hair and beard. That's really all I can remember."

Something in his statement caught Steve's attention. "Wait. Did you say Saturday morning?"

The cashier nodded. "Yeah. Probably sometime around eight or nine."

"Okay, thanks for your help." Steve gave a quick wave and turned to leave the store.

Matt and Jenny followed.

Once outside, Steve faced his friends. "Did you hear that? The man pawned the things on Saturday morning."

Bending down, Matt picked up his bike. "What's the big deal?"

"The big deal is that Rosa and her dad left Friday night. That means the robbery had to have happened either really late Friday or early Saturday morning. Whoever did this had to have been watching the house to know when it would be safe. That proves our theory that this wasn't an accident. He broke in, messed the house up, and then got rid of his stolen decoys fast before they were reported missing."

Matt's phone chimed. He checked the text. "I gotta go. Text me and let me know what time we're meeting tomorrow."

Splitting up, each kid headed home, agreeing to talk later and discuss a plan of action.

After dinner, Steve helped his parents set up a new laptop then retreated to his bedroom. Rosa had texted and asked them to come to her house at ten in the morning. Matt and Jenny agreed to meet at Steve's home first, then the three of them would ride over to Rosa's together.

Reclining in his bed, Steve pulled up the picture of the music box that Rosa had sent him. What was so important about that box that a burglar would be willing to ransack a house to throw off the police investigation?

He used his fingers to zoom the picture. The music box appeared to be somewhat fuzzy, like worn-out red velvet, with unraveling gold threading all over. The front of the box had a simple gold lock, but what caught Steve's attention were the designs on each side. They looked as though they had been added on, after the fact. The image on the left of the lock had two black lightning bolts, and the one on the right had a red square with a white plus sign inside it.

Steve frowned. The red square and white plus sign seemed familiar. He did a Google search and the results brought up the flag of Switzerland. He bit his lip. Perhaps the music box came from Switzerland.

Next, he did a search for the side by side black lightning bolts. When the monitor displayed the results, his eyes widened with surprise. Dual black lightning bolts were a symbol of the *Schutzstaffel*, or the SS, Adolf Hitler's elite paramilitary force.

Steve leaned back in his bed and stared up at the ceiling, a million questions racing through his head. Why would the music box have both SS and Swiss symbols on it? What did they mean? Why did the grandfather have this box in the first place? And why did he say that inside was the key to great fortune when he knew it had nothing in it?

2 THE MUSIC BOX

At ten o'clock exactly, Steve rang the doorbell of Rosa's house. She answered and invited the Decoders in.

"Please excuse the mess. We did not have time to fix things."

As they made their way through the living room, Steve took a good look at the interior of the home. Overturned furniture lay about the floor, and papers had been thrown everywhere, just as she had described yesterday. But something bothered him. Although he believed the mess to be a distraction for the police, the papers on the floor were unusual. He bent down for a closer examination. Several pieces of mail appeared to have been deliberately opened and separated from their envelopes.

"Rosa," he said as he stood, "where exactly did you have the music box?"

She pointed to the hallway. "It was in my bedroom. Follow me." They walked to the room at the end of the hall. Inside, to the left of the twin-sized bed, stood a small nightstand. She pointed to it.

"I kept it there, next to my bed. I wanted to keep it near me."

Steve studied the surroundings. Across from her bed, against the wall, was a chest of drawers. On top lay a small television and a jewelry box. He pointed to the box. "I'm surprised the burglar didn't take that."

Rosa put her hand over her heart and closed her eyes. "Yes. We were fortunate. My mother's wedding ring and her favorite bracelets are in there. She died when I was born, so that is all I have of hers."

"You are *so* lucky they weren't stolen," Jenny said. "You should hide those somewhere safe, so no one sees them. My mom died when I was little, too. I keep her wedding ring in one of my shoes, just in case."

Opening her eyes, the dark-haired girl nodded. "That is a good idea. I will do that later today."

Jenny shook her head. "I'd feel better about it if we did it right now."

With Matt's help, the two girls began rearranging things in the closet, trying to decide on the best hiding place.

Steve didn't pay much attention to their movements. He walked out and returned to the living room. Something still nagged at him. Rosa had sent him a list of the items that had been stolen. As he peered around, there were several things a thief would have taken had they simply been hoping for quick cash. The most obvious being the Wii system sitting by the TV. No crook would leave that. The more he looked around, the more it confirmed his theory of the music box being the target.

He bent down and sorted through some of the thrown papers and envelopes. Why would the thief take the time to search the mail? Steve bit his lip in thought. Perhaps the burglar wanted a specific piece of mail, something the Romeros had received. Something important. That could explain the overturned furniture as well. Whatever the thief had been searching for, he must have thought the Romeros had hidden it somewhere in the house.

Just then, the front door opened and a man walked in. Not very tall, he had thick black hair and a pencil-thin moustache. Steve recognized him immediately as Rosa's father. She looked just like him.

"Hello, Mr. Romero. I'm Steve Kemp, a friend of Rosa's."

The dad smiled and nodded. "Yes, she said some of her friends would be coming with us.

Thank you for being here. Today will be hard for her. She and her grandfather were very close."

Rosa, Matt, and Jenny joined them in the living room. After introductions, Mr. Romero excused himself and promised they would be leaving in five minutes.

Once he left the room, Steve turned to Rosa. "I noticed a lot of mail on the floor. Do you know if any of it is missing?"

Rosa appeared surprised. "Why would the thief take our mail?"

Bending down to examine an envelope near her foot, Jenny replied, "Sometimes thieves hit mailboxes to do identity theft. Are you guys missing any new credit or debit cards?"

The Mexican girl shook her head. "My father has no cards at all. He prefers to pay with cash."

Steve scrunched his forehead in thought. This had to be more than just identity theft. "What about other mail? Did you guys receive anything important lately? It seems like the burglar went to a lot of trouble going through every single piece of paper. Could there have been something special that they'd be looking for?"

Rosa shrugged. "No, there is nothing. We do not get much mail, not even from family. We mostly use Skype and Facebook."

Just then, her father returned, and the group left the house.

Steve rode in silence on the way to the nursing home. The burglar had been searching for something specific. Although Rosa didn't know what it could be, her father most likely did. But Steve couldn't ask him about it. Rosa made them promise not to tell her dad that she had hired them to find the music box. She said he would be furious if he found out, and that he wanted to just forget about the robbery and move on.

Once inside the nursing home, they split up. Mr. Romero went to talk to the front office staff about the grandfather's belongings, while Rosa and the kids went to see the room he had stayed in.

As they walked inside, they stopped short. A man lay on the bed and looked at them curiously.

"Sorry," Rosa said quickly and backed out of the doorway. "I didn't know someone was here."

It had been two weeks since her grandfather passed away, so it made sense that the room would have a new occupant.

Trying to decide what to do next, the kids stood talking in the hallway when a pretty, blonde nurse walked by. Rosa stopped her.

"Excuse me, is Nurse Karl here? I would like to talk to him."

The young woman shook her head. "Sorry, but Karl quit."

Rosa's eyebrows shot up. "Nurse Karl is gone?"

Crossing her arms, the nurse nodded. "Yep, just like that. One day he was here, the next day he called and said he wasn't coming back. Now all of us are scrambling trying to cover his shifts." She sounded irritated.

"When did he quit?" Steve asked.

The woman's eyes narrowed as if trying to remember. "Maybe two weeks ago. I don't recall exactly."

"Okay, thanks," Steve said.

After watching the nurse walk away, Rosa sighed heavily. "I cannot believe Nurse Karl is gone. Grandfather loved him. He was the only nurse that would stay with him for hours, listening to his stories. Sometimes, he would come in on his day off just to take care of grandfather. He was a very nice man."

As the kids walked slowly back to the main lobby, Steve processed the new information. Nurse Karl had quit two weeks ago, right around the same time her grandfather died. Could that be a coincidence?

"Rosa!" Mr. Romero's voice interrupted his thoughts.

The kids turned around and saw the man waving them over. "Could you and your friends help me carry these things to the car?"

They all agreed and each grabbed a box. Once the car had been packed, they returned to the

Romero house and helped their new friends unload the trunk and place all of the boxes in the living room.

After saying good-bye to Mr. Romero, the kids walked to the front door. Steve turned the doorknob then paused. "Rosa, do you by any chance know Nurse Karl's last name?"

She nodded. "Yes. His name is Karl Schmidt. Why?"

"Just curious." He opened the door. "We'll keep you posted on our progress."

The trio hopped on their bikes and began the trek back to Steve's house.

"So, why'd you want to know Nurse Karl's last name?" Jenny asked.

Making sure no cars were coming, Steve turned onto the main road. "Because I think he might be able to help us. Rosa said that he spent a lot of time with her grandfather. Perhaps he can remember something the older man said about the music box. Something that could help us find it."

Matt's bike skidded. "Whoa. Watch out for those rocks. Hold on, I don't get it. How can something the old guy said two weeks ago help us find the box now?"

"Because," Steve said, "I believe the box was stolen for a specific reason. A really important one."

"Like what?" Jenny asked.

Steve pulled into his driveway and eased his

bike on the grass. "I think it has something to do with Nazi Germany."

After dropping his bicycle next to Steve's, Matt put a finger in his ear as though cleaning it out. "Say that again. I'm pretty sure I didn't hear you right."

As he reached into his pocket to take out his house key, Steve repeated his last statement. "I think the music box has something to do with Nazi Germany."

Matt shook his head. "Yep. That's what I thought you said."

"What makes you think that?" Jenny asked.

He unlocked the door. "Because the front of it had a design of two black lightning bolts, the symbol of the SS."

Once all three were inside, Matt closed the door behind them. "What's the SS?"

Steve led them into the living room and sat on the sofa. He pulled out his cell phone. "The SS were Hitler's elite military group. They started out as his personal bodyguards, the ones he trusted the most, then grew into a bigger organization."

Sitting cross-legged on the floor, Jenny untied her hair from the rubber band. "Why would Rosa's grandfather have a Nazi music box? He wasn't German, he was Mexican."

Matt grabbed an apple from the fruit basket in the nearby kitchen before joining Steve on the couch. He wiped it with his shirt then took a bite. "Maybe he moved to Mexico as a little kid."

Steve typed something into his phone. "No. Didn't you see the picture of the three of them in their house?"

Both Jenny and Matt shook their heads.

Steve sighed. "We really need to work on your powers of observation. There was a photograph of the three of them standing at the Beachdale Pier, obviously not taken that long ago. Her grandfather had dark skin, like Rosa. German people are light skinned."

While braiding her hair, Jenny frowned. "So, back to my original question, why would Rosa's grandfather have a Nazi music box?"

"That's something I'm hoping Nurse Karl can tell us." He held up his phone. "And now that we have his home address, I suggest we go pay him a visit."

Matt's eyes widened. "We're gonna stalk him?"

Rolling his eyes, Steve stood. "Not stalk him. Talk to him. We'll just say we're friends of Rosa's and tell him about the stolen music box. If he was as close to the grandfather as Rosa said, he'll want to help."

Jenny jumped up. "I'm in."

Matt stuffed a large bite of apple in his mouth. "Mmph too."

The kids laughed as pieces of apple flew out of Matt's mouth, making him laugh harder, causing more apple pieces to fly out, and causing all of them to laugh harder.

After cleaning up the apple mess, the trio walked over to the bus stop. Nurse Karl did not live in Beachdale, but in the nearby town of Sommersby, too far to go by bicycle.

The bus ride went fast and soon the three kids were on foot, following their phone's GPS to their destination. Within fifteen minutes, they found the address.

Steve took mental notes of the premises. The front yard needed serious maintenance. The lawn had become overgrown and the bushes needed trimming. The small white house appeared to be in decent shape although it could use a new coat of paint. The front porch had a wooden bench that, like the house, needed painting.

Walking up, Matt rang the doorbell. No answer. He waited about thirty seconds then rang again. Nothing.

Steve cleared his throat. "Hello? We're looking for Karl Schmidt." He waited a few seconds. "Nurse Karl? We're friends with Rosa Romero. We have a few questions about her grandfather."

No response.

Matt shrugged. "I guess no one's home."

Steve said nothing. He walked to the left side

of the house. One of the windows had the curtains open. Steve went up to it.

"Dude," Matt said in a loud whisper behind him. "What are you doing? We can't just look into people's homes."

Pushing Matt to the side, Jenny disagreed. "Why not? It's not like anyone's here. We rang the doorbell."

Steve took a peek inside the house. The window belonged to a bedroom. He scanned the room quickly and his eyes widened. "You guys need to see this."

Obviously nervous, Matt glanced around. "Okay, one quick look and then we should go."

Jenny grabbed his arm. "No way. Matt, check it out!"

He peeked inside and his jaw dropped. "Is that…"

"Rosa's music box," Steve finished.

Jenny smacked her forehead with her hand. "I can't believe it. Nurse Karl is the thief?"

Biting his lip, Steve shook his head. "We have no proof of that. He could've gotten it from someone else." He paused as he began walking toward the front of the house. "Or, it might not even be the same music box. We need to get a better look at it."

"And how do you suggest we do that?" Matt said. "Wait." He stopped walking and glanced around again. "Please tell me you're not thinking of breaking in. You know that's illegal, right? We'd get like fifty years in prison with nothing to eat but bread crumbs and sauerkraut."

"Bread crumbs and sauerkraut?" Jenny repeated. "Where do you get these things?"

Reaching the front door, Steve surveyed the area. "Relax," he said and bent down. He lifted the welcome mat, checked underneath, and then put it back.

"What's he doing?" Matt asked Jenny.

"I seriously have no idea."

After moving his hands into the nearby potted plant, Steve paused for a moment, then grinned. "Aha!" He held up a key for the other two to see.

Matt groaned. "We're going to jail for sure."

Steve put the key into the handle and turned it. The door creaked open.

As quietly as possible, the trio crept into the house and shut the door behind them.

"Okay," Matt whispered, "Let's do this quick and get out of here fast."

Moving silently into the bedroom, they crowded around the music box. Determining it to be identical to Rosa's, Steve opened it up and the three detectives peered inside. There, in bold black letters, were the words ROSA ROMERO and a date.

Steve looked at his friends and they both

nodded. No mistaking it, Nurse Karl had Rosa's missing music box.

"Now what?" Matt asked. "I mean, it's not like we can just walk out with it."

"Why not?" Jenny demanded. "It's Rosa's box. He stole it, the little thief!"

Steve could tell by the escalation in Jenny's voice that her temper was rising. He needed to calm her down.

"Hold on," he said in a soothing voice. "We have to think about this logically. If Nurse Karl comes home and finds the box missing, he might go after Rosa and her dad, thinking they might have something to do with it. That could put them in danger."

"That's true," Jenny said, her voice sounding a bit calmer.

"So then, what should we do?" Matt asked.

Steve thought for a moment. "I suggest we—"

He froze.

The crunch of heavy footsteps sounded outside. Then, the worst noise ever. Someone put a key into the front doorknob.

"Hide!" Steve whispered frantically.

3 NAZI GOLD

The kids sprang into action. Steve opened the closet and crouched underneath the clothes, sliding the door shut in front of him. Matt ran into the bathroom, climbed into the bathtub, and pulled the shower curtain closed. Jenny squirmed underneath the bed.

Steve held his breath. The sound of the front door opening and closing filled the house. Keys jingled and thumped, probably thrown onto the front table. The boy exhaled but tried to keep his breathing slow and quiet even though his heart raced uncontrollably in his chest. In all reality, they had no idea how dangerous this man was.

Footsteps echoed on the carpet close by. Someone had entered the bedroom. Cold sweat ran down Steve's face as he held his breath again. Any moment now, he could be caught.

A cell phone ring interrupted his thoughts.

"*Ja?*" a man's voice sounded.

Making a quick decision, Steve pulled the cell from his pocket. The closet door stood about an inch open. He hit the video button and then placed the phone near the opening, hoping to catch the man's image. Perhaps later, they could show the video to Rosa and have her identify Nurse Karl for sure.

The man grunted. "Very well. I'll be there in ten minutes."

Footsteps resonated again, but this time they grew softer. Steve exhaled slowly. The clatter of the front door opening and closing filled the house again.

He waited about fifteen seconds before sliding the closet door open, then peeked out. Nothing. He crawled forward and stood.

"Is it safe?" Jenny's whisper came from under the bed. She peered up at Steve.

After taking a quick look into the living room, he gave a thumb's up. "Yeah, he's gone."

Matt walked in from the bathroom. "Okay, dudes, my heart seriously cannot take much more of this. I'm like a stress mess."

"Do you think that was Nurse Karl?" Jenny asked as she stood and smoothed out her shirt.

"I don't know." Steve played the video he had taken. He paused it on a frame where the man had his face toward the closet. "Does this guy seem familiar?" He showed them the picture.

Matt gave a short laugh. "White guy, kinda chubby, with reddish-brown hair and beard."

Jenny clasped her hands together. "This is the guy who pawned off Rosa's things."

Putting his cell back into his pocket, Steve nodded. "We found the thief, no doubt about that. I'm just not certain if this man is actually Nurse Karl."

"So, what should we do now?" Matt asked.

Jenny whipped out the cell phone from her back pocket. "We call the cops, that's what. This guy is going down, and I for one want to be there when he does."

Steve held up his hands in a 'slow down' gesture. "Hold on a second. We need to go about this logically. We can't call the cops from here. We shouldn't even be inside of this house."

Jenny shrugged. "Fine. Then we'll step outside and call from there."

"And tell them what?" Steve asked. "That we see a music box through the window that looks just like the one a friend of ours had stolen from her house a few days ago? The police would never take us seriously."

"We could call Tyrone," Matt suggested. "Maybe he'll call the cops for us. He's done it before."

Steve shook his head. "I don't want—" He froze. The front door sounded again. "He's back. Hide!"

Panicking, the three detectives quickly moved to their original hiding spots. Steve heard the front door open and close, just like last time. Perhaps Nurse Karl had forgotten something. Steve prayed whatever he came back for was not in the closet or under the bed.

Footsteps sounded close by. The man had entered the bedroom.

Holding his breath, Steve pushed record on his phone again and put it up to the closet opening.

Moments later, the footsteps disappeared and Steve heard the clang of the front door again. After waiting a few seconds, he slid the closet door open and peeked out. No one. He stood and prepared to call out to Matt and Jenny when he noticed something wrong.

Crawling out from underneath the bed, Jenny appeared to also notice it right away. "No!"

"What's wrong?" Matt asked as he walked in from the bathroom.

"Nurse Karl took the music box with him." Jenny's voice sounded upset.

Steve stared at the image on his phone and hit play. Frowning, he watched the video again to be sure. "Guys, take a look at this."

After pressing play, he watched his friends'

faces. Both Matt and Jenny appeared as surprised as he had been.

When the video finished, Matt turned to Steve. "That wasn't the same guy."

Steve studied the image on his phone. "No, it was not. And now this mystery man has the music box."

Jenny crossed her arms and stomped her foot. "What in the world is so special about this box?"

Moving toward the front door, Steve shrugged. "I don't know. But if we plan on helping Rosa, we've got to figure that out. But first, I suggest we get out of here before anyone else decides to show up."

"No argument there," Matt said.

Once outside, the kids began their walk to the bus stop.

"So, what's the plan now?" Jenny asked.

Steve took out his cell. "We call in the big guns." He dialed Alysha's number, pushed the speakerphone button, and explained the situation to her. A whiz on the internet, Alysha could always find information on pretty much any topic, no matter how obscure.

"I'll see what I can come up with. Can you guys come by around seven?"

All three kids said yes.

After hanging up, Steve bit his lip. They were so close to getting the box, only to have it taken from right in front of them. "I wish I knew who that mystery guy was."

Matt nodded. "Me, too. Do you think he knows Nurse Karl? I mean, he had a key, so I'm guessing he must know him."

Bending down, Jenny re-tied her shoelace that had loosened during their ordeal. "But if he knew him, then why sneak in and steal the music box? If they're friends, he wouldn't just come in and take it when his buddy wasn't home."

Matt shrugged. "Maybe that Nurse Karl dude asked him to go to his house and get the box. They could be in on this together. What do you think, Steve?"

He thought for a moment before answering. "Nurse Karl, or whoever the first guy was, had only been gone for five minutes before the mystery man came in. If I had to guess, I'd say he waited around for him to leave before making his move. I don't think they're working together. But one thing I do know, there's more to this music box than Rosa knows."

After dinner, Steve helped his mom with the dishes then walked down the hallway to his bedroom to grab his backpack. If only they knew the identity of the mystery man, then they could figure out not only where the missing music box was, but also why everyone wanted it so badly.

As he biked to Alysha's, he tried to put the pieces together in his mind. Nurse Karl had befriended Rosa's grandfather. Could that have been on purpose? Had it always been his intention to get the music box? Or, was it a coincidence? Had he learned about the box from the grandfather and then decided to steal it?

He reached Alysha's house just as Matt pulled up. They dropped their bikes near the front and rang the bell. The door opened and Alysha's mom, a petite woman in her mid-forties, greeted them. "Come on in, boys. She's waiting for you in the study."

They thanked her and made their way down the extra-wide hallway toward their friend. Like all the rooms in the house, the study had a low doorknob and a grab bar on the wall next to the door.

As soon as they walked in, Alysha turned her wheelchair around to greet them, and her green eyes lit up. It was common knowledge at Beachdale Middle School that Alysha Stonestreet had a huge crush on Steve.

"Hey, Steve. Hey, Matt." She pushed her strawberry blonde hair back. "Can you give me just a few more minutes?"

"No problem." Matt plopped down on the couch and leaned forward to examine the candy bowl on the coffee table

Ten minutes later, Jenny walked in and sat on

the sofa between the two boys. "Sorry I'm late. Dad needed help with something, and it took longer than I thought." Jenny's father owned a repair shop, and Jenny, who was great at fixing things herself, often helped him out.

"No big," Matt said as he fished through the candies for green M&Ms.

Alysha rolled her wheelchair over to the sofa. "Okay, I'm not sure if I'm on the right track, but I may have found something." She flipped through several pages of printer paper. "First of all, there's nothing anywhere on the internet about a music box with SS and Swiss symbols on it. I did, however, find several references to the SS and Switzerland. Apparently, throughout World War II, a top general in the SS, along with a group of his officers, had begun smuggling gold out of Germany and depositing it in safety deposit boxes inside a Swiss bank that Hitler couldn't touch."

Matt pulled a green chocolate piece out of the dish. "Hold on. I thought the SS were Hitler's most trusted men." He tossed the M&M up in the air and caught it in his mouth.

Alysha nodded. "They were. Except in this case, this particular general used his position to make himself, and his officer friends, rich. Unfortunately for him, Hitler found out and had him executed."

"So what happened to the gold?" Jenny asked.

Leaning back, the girl shrugged. "That is one of the great mysteries of World War II. Several years after the war ended, officials in the new German government got permission from the Swiss government to claim the gold in those safety deposit boxes. But when they opened up the boxes, they were empty. All the gold was missing."

Matt interlocked his hands behind his neck and rested his head back. "How much gold are we talking about here? I mean, safety deposit boxes aren't that big, right? So, what're we thinking? A couple dozen coins, maybe? That'd be pretty easy to smuggle out of there."

Alysha laughed and shook her head. "Try about thirty gold bars. They make safety deposit boxes in all sizes. And just so you understand, each gold bar, in today's money, would be worth about five hundred thousand dollars."

Hunching forward, elbows on his knees, Matt whistled. "Five hundred thousand bucks? Times thirty? That's like...like...like a whole lot of money."

"Fifteen million dollars to be exact," Steve said.

Jenny frowned. "I still don't understand. What does this gold have to do with the music box?"

Alysha sighed. "Possibly nothing. But this story is the only one I found that directly links the SS to Switzerland. And so you know how much crazier this story gets, in the last fifteen years, the Neo-Nazis have offered a reward for anyone who can give them a clue to this missing gold. They claim it's rightfully theirs."

Matt frowned. "Who are the Neo-Nazis?"

"Neo is simply a prefix meaning new," Steve explained. "It's just a fancy way to say they are the modern Nazi Party."

Flipping through the papers in her hands, Alysha nodded. "I did some reading on them. They're found mostly in Germany, even though there are small cells of them scattered around the world, even here in the United States."

"Better not let me find any of them," Matt mumbled.

"They're pretty well connected, mostly due to the internet," Alysha continued. "But they lack funding. Most of their big money suppliers are dying off."

Scrunching his forehead in thought, Steve processed the new information. "And fifteen million dollars would be a big help to their cause. If that music box is somehow a clue to the missing gold, then it makes sense that a bunch of different people are after it."

Tilting her head to the side, Jenny looked confused. "Then what was Rosa's grandfather doing with it in the first place? Do you think he knew?"

Steve nodded slowly. "I would bet on it.

Remember what he told her when he gave it to her? He said that inside was the key to great fortune. He must've been talking about the gold."

"But how would he know about it?" Matt asked.

Steve shrugged. "I'm not certain, but I think tomorrow we should pay Rosa another visit. We need to learn everything we can about her grandfather, and not just what he did once he moved here. Something in his past is the secret to solving this mystery."

After texting Rosa back and forth, Steve made plans to drop by her house the next day at noon. Jenny had to help her father in the shop again, and Matt had promised his mother that he would help clean out the garage, so Steve would be on his own. The three friends agreed to meet up in the afternoon.

That night, as Steve lay in bed, he contemplated their new theory. If Nurse Karl and the mystery man were both after the gold, then they both could be very dangerous. He decided not to tell Rosa about what had happened at Nurse Karl's house. Rosa seemed like a very sweet girl, but she also gave the impression of someone extremely cautious. She may not want the detectives to put themselves in danger over a music box.

Instead, he would tell her about the gold theory

and see if she could shed some light on her grandfather's past. The elderly man had acquired the box at some point in his life, and he knew its secret. Somehow, the Decoders needed to figure out that secret before anyone else did, and before anyone got hurt.

4 THE MUSEUM

At noon exactly, Steve rang the doorbell. A few moments later, Rosa answered and invited him in.

As they walked toward the living room sofa, Steve noticed that much of the mess had been cleaned up. All the papers had been placed into piles on the dining room table, and all the furniture had been restored to its upright position.

Rosa sat cross-legged on the couch with Steve facing her. He explained what Alysha had found out about the missing SS gold in Switzerland and their theory about the music box being connected to it.

Pushing a strand of black hair behind her ears, Rosa seemed surprised. "I can't believe that box could be a clue to a missing treasure. It doesn't feel possible."

Steve pulled out his cell. "It's just a theory right now, but we want to follow every lead that we can. If other people have this idea as well, it may help us find who stole your music box." He opened the app containing his notes. "What I want to do now is ask you a few questions about your grandfather. Do you know where he got the music box?"

She shook her head. "No. A few months ago, he brought it home with him one day after work. And when he moved into the nursing home, he asked us to bring it to him."

As he typed her responses into his phone, he bit his lip in thought. Those actions confirmed his belief that her grandfather knew the significance of the box. "Tell me a little more about him—where he was born, where he went to school, if he travelled a lot, anything you can think of."

Leaning back into the couch, Rosa took a deep breath. "My grandfather was born in Queretaro, Mexico. He studied history and geology at the University of Mexico." She paused and laughed. "He was a funny man. He liked to do…how you say…pranks. They almost kicked him out of the university twice because of this." She laughed again.

Steve smiled. Her grandfather sounded a lot like his own grandpa.

He looked up from his phone. "Did he work or travel when he got out of college?"

She thought for a moment. "He went to work at

a museum as soon as he graduated. That is where he met my grandmother. She worked there also. They were married and two years later, they had my father."

"Is that the same museum he worked at before he moved here?"

She nodded. "Yes. Grandfather worked at the Museo de Reliquias Históricas for forty years. I don't think he would ever have moved here if the museum had not closed."

If he worked at that museum for so long, perhaps the music box came from there. Then other people who worked there could also know about it. That would be something they might need to look into. Steve typed into his phone. "And your grandmother? Does she still live in Mexico?"

An expression of sadness covered her face. "No. She died a few days after having my father. I never got to meet her, but my grandfather says I look just like her."

Steve cleared his throat. "I'm sorry about your grandmother. My dad's mom died when I was little and my mom's mom lives in New York, so I don't get to see her very much. I'm glad you got to know your grandpa as well as you did. Did you and your dad live in the same city as him back in Mexico?"

She smiled. "Yes, in the same house. My mom and I took care of the house while my father and grandfather went to work."

"Did your father work for the museum, too?"

She shook her head. "No, he worked for the telephone company."

After checking an incoming text from Matt complaining about the amount of junk his mom had collected in the garage, Steve continued typing into his notes. "Why did your family decide to move here?"

Playing with the ring on her finger, the girl blinked several times and tears swelled in her eyes. "My mother became sick. When she died, my dad became very sad. He did not want to live in the same house because it made him cry every day. We have an aunt who lives in San Diego, so we moved to the United States. We lived with her for a few months until my father got a job here in Beachdale."

Steve watched the girl fiddle with the ring. "Did that ring belong to your mother?"

She looked up. "How did you know?"

"It's beautiful, yet a little too big for you, but too small to be a man's ring. Therefore, it must've belonged to a woman. Because you started playing with it when talking about your mom, I deduced it was hers."

Brushing a tear off her cheek, Rosa smiled. "You are very smart. I think you will find my music box."

Just then, her father walked through the front door. He greeted the two kids then said something

45

to Rosa in Spanish. Steve only understood the word *tienda*, which meant store.

As the man disappeared into the hallway, Rosa sighed. "I have to go shopping with my father now. I hope I have told you something good."

After returning the phone to his pocket, Steve stood and walked to the front door. "It was all very helpful. If I think of any more questions, I'll text you."

She nodded and smiled shyly. "Good. And maybe next time we can all meet, Matt and Jenny as well."

Steve agreed and said good bye. As he rode his bike down the street, he glanced at his watch. There were still over two hours before the other Decoders planned to meet him at his house, plenty of time for a visit to the museum. Rosa said that her grandfather had transferred some of the artifacts from his museum to this one. Perhaps, something there would give more insight into her grandfather's life.

Reaching his destination a little after one o'clock, he showed his student ID to get free admission, then grabbed a map and headed to a nearby bench. After a few moments of studying the brochure, he determined that in order to see her grandfather's artifacts, he would need to go to the second floor, not far from the Magic Sapphire. Steve smiled as he read the name. The Magic

Sapphire had been their first case as detectives. Although he couldn't explain it, Steve had some kind of mental connection to the stone.

Climbing the stairs, he made his way to the World War II exhibit. He read the information tags on all the artifacts and found the ones brought there from Mexico. There were several impressive items from World War II including a German rifle and footlocker, a French resistance uniform, and an American Red Cross package made to be given to American POWs.

Suddenly, he heard whispering. He glanced around but saw no one in the area. The Magic Sapphire was calling him, just like it had on their first case. He could feel that the stone wanted him to go to it. He left the World War II exhibit and wandered into the rare gems room. There it sat, a bright blue sapphire the size of a man's fist.

No other visitors lingered inside the room. Steve walked up and touched the glass. He could hear the whispering in his head, but he couldn't understand it. He stepped back and the muffled sounds changed, as though coming from behind him. He turned around and the murmuring seemed to be located outside the room.

He exited, heard the mumbles coming from his right, then realized the Sapphire was guiding him somewhere. He followed the sound and within minutes came to a wall. The whispering stopped.

Numerous pictures of the World War II exhibit from the Museo de Reliquias Históricas, Rosa's grandfather's museum, covered the wall. He studied each photograph thoroughly. When he came to one near the end of the exhibit, his eyes widened. He took out his phone and snapped a picture. Matt and Jenny had to see this.

Steve waited impatiently for his friends to arrive. This picture changed everything. Finally, at three o'clock, the two of them walked in the front door.

"I thought you guys would never get here." Steve led them to the family room sofa.

"Dude, relax," Matt said as he and Jenny plopped down on the couch. "Jenny's dad just needed a little more time to finish his project."

"That's okay." Steve turned the laptop sitting on the coffee table to face them. "Take a look at this."

The two friends studied the image on the screen.

"No...way," Jenny managed to say.

Matt pointed. "Dude, is that who I think it is?"

Steve nodded. "That is a picture of Rosa's grandfather and our mystery man, posing at the World War II exhibit in Mexico."

Jenny turned to Steve. "That means that Rosa's grandfather knew the man who took the music box from Nurse Karl!"

Steve tapped the screen. "Look again. Check out the background."

Matt squinted at the monitor, then his eyes widened. "Whoa! That's the music box!"

"It was part of the exhibit in Mexico," Jenny said.

Turning the monitor toward himself, Steve nodded. "My guess is that after moving here with all those artifacts, Rosa's grandfather discovered the connection of the music box to the missing SS gold. I asked the guy at the museum if people who donated items could retrieve them, and he said yes."

Jenny raised her knees and wrapped her arms around them. "So, Rosa's grandfather asked the museum if he could bring the music box home so he could study it, but then he got sick."

After pulling an ottoman closer, Matt placed his feet on top of it. "Then he took the music box with him to the nursing home, probably thinking he could work on the mystery there, but then he started losing his memory."

Steve shut down the computer. "And when he died, the guy in the photograph must have wanted to get the music box to solve the mystery himself. He must have tracked down Nurse Karl the same way we did."

"But...who exactly *is* the guy in the picture?" Jenny asked.

Steve shrugged. "I don't know. I texted the

photo to Rosa to see if she could identify him, but she hasn't responded yet."

"Hey, yeah," Matt said. "Tell us what happened at Rosa's."

"And don't leave anything out." Jenny's eyes twinkled. "We wouldn't want Matt to get jealous of you."

Matt's face turned slightly red. "What? Why would I get jealous?"

Jenny laughed. "Seriously? You are like so into her."

"No, I'm not," Matt said defensively.

Whipping out his cell before their conversation got out of control, Steve opened his notes and cleared his throat. "Okay, here's the breakdown of what I learned." He proceeded to fill his friends in on everything Rosa had told him earlier.

Matt leaned back into the couch. "Wait. If this mystery guy and Rosa's grandfather worked at the museum together, Rosa probably knows him."

Steve agreed. "I hope so. That would make tracking down the box easier if we knew who to look for. We'll know more once we get in touch with Rosa."

Matt frowned. "What I still don't get is how Nurse Karl fits into this."

"Yeah," Jenny said. "If he was just a worker at the nursing home, what would he be doing breaking into Rosa's house and stealing the music box?"

After putting his cell away, Steve leaned back and crossed his arms. "What if his job was just a cover?"

"What do you mean?" Matt asked.

"What if Karl became a nurse just to get close to Rosa's grandfather? Think about it. He got the job around the same time the Romeros admitted him to the nursing home, and then when the elderly man died, Karl stopped showing up for work."

Matt held up his hand. "Hold up. That would mean that Nurse Karl knew about the music box ahead of time."

Steve nodded. "Exactly."

Beeping filled the air. Matt checked the text on his phone. "Mom wants me home for dinner." He stood. "I gotta go."

After checking the time on her cell, Jenny followed. "Yeah, I should probably get home, too."

Steve walked his friends to the front door. "Do either of you have plans for tomorrow?" After they both said no, he continued. "Meet me here at ten in the morning. We've got some investigating to do."

After dinner, Steve watched TV with his parents until nine o'clock, then went to his bedroom and turned on his laptop.

He checked his cell and noticed he had received a text from Rosa. She recognized the man in the photograph as Saul Mendoza, another docent at the Museo de Reliquias Históricas. Rosa remembered seeing him a few times at their house in Mexico. Steve frowned. If Saul had been a friend of Rosa's grandfather, then why wouldn't he have received the music box after the man died? Why give the box to Rosa?

He pulled up the picture of Saul Mendoza and texted it to Tyrone, asking if he knew anything about him. Besides owning the best diner in Beachdale, Tyrone was also the best source of information of everything happening in town. The man replied within seconds, saying he didn't recognize him but that he'd check into it.

Returning to his laptop, Steve did a search for Museo de Reliquias Históricas. The first result turned out to be a Wikipedia entry. He read through it but didn't find anything useful.

He went back and scanned the results. A particular one caught his eye—a newspaper article from three years earlier. Although written in Spanish, the article held a few words Steve could identify. After struggling a few moments longer, he finally copied the entire thing and pasted it into Google Translate.

Upon reading through the translation, Steve sat up. According to the article, the museum had housed some of Germany's most infamous artifacts, including scepters and daggers used by the SS. The music box allegedly belonged to one of the SS's top officials, Alois Schultz. At the end of World War II, many German officers attempted to flee the country, including Schultz. But he was captured and killed by a gang of angry German soldiers, who accused him of being a traitor.

Steve leaned back and bit his lip. If Schultz had been one of the original officers smuggling gold out of Germany, then he could've been on his way to retrieve it, but got caught instead. That would mean he never reached the Swiss bank to withdraw the gold. So then, who did?

He yawned and closed his computer. Perhaps, in the morning, all this would start to make sense.

At seven o'clock, his cell phone rang.

"Hello?" he answered groggily.

"Steve? It's Alysha."

He yawned. "What's up?"

"The museum was robbed last night."

Steve jumped up in bed. "What? What happened?"

"Someone broke into the museum and stole a bunch of stuff from the World War II exhibit."

His jaw dropped. "And the stuff that Rosa's grandfather had donated?"

"All gone."

No way could this be a coincidence. "Thanks for calling."

"No problem. I figured you'd want to know."

After they hung up, Steve stared at the ceiling.

Why would thieves steal the museum's artifacts? The music box was no longer there, and hadn't been for a while. What could they have been after?

5 TRAPPED!

Leaping up, Steve crossed the room to get his laptop and returned to bed. Pulling up the picture from the museum wall, he zoomed in and studied the background carefully. Besides the music box, there were several other objects. One of them had to hold another clue.

A knock on the door distracted him. "Steve? Are you awake?"

"Yeah, Mom. What's up?"

"Could you help your father and I outside for a moment? We need a third pair of hands."

"Sure. Give me a sec to get dressed."

He shut down his computer, but his mind could not stop thinking about the museum robbery. What were they looking for?

At ten o'clock, Steve opened the door allowing

Matt and Jenny into the house. They made their way over to the living room sofa.

Matt opened a granola bar he had pulled out of his pocket. "What's the plan, chief?"

Steve relayed the news about the museum robbery.

"No way," Jenny said. "What do you think they wanted from there?"

"And who do you think did it?" Matt asked in-between bites. "Nurse Karl or our mystery man?"

Steve leaned back on the couch. "Rosa texted last night. The man in the photograph is Saul Mendoza. He worked with her grandfather at the museum in Mexico."

Jenny frowned. "Why would this Mendoza guy steal the music box?"

After wadding the wrapper in his hands, Matt walked over to the nearby garbage can and threw away his trash. "Maybe he's after the gold. He could've tried to get the music box from Rosa's grandpa, and when he wouldn't give it to him, he waited until he could take it. But Nurse Karl beat him to it." He returned to the sofa and plopped down.

Jenny sat on crossed legs. "So, why rob the museum? What could he have been searching for there?"

Steve scrunched his forehead. "There's a piece to this puzzle that we're missing. I suggest we return to Nurse Karl's house and take a good look around. Perhaps we can find a clue to help us out."

As she tied her long hair in a bun, Jenny agreed with Steve's idea. "It's also possible that Karl is the museum thief. We might find the stolen stuff at his house, too."

Matt held up his hands and shook his head. "Are you two nuts? The dude's a thief. Who knows what he'll do to us if he finds us there."

"Which is why we'll need you to be the lookout while Jenny and I search the house," Steve said.

"I'm in," Jenny said.

Matt still appeared unsure.

"It'll be fine," Steve said assuredly. "Nurse Karl's street ends in a cul-de-sac, so he could only be driving up from one direction. You can be watching for him, and if you see him, call our cells and we'll go out the back door and hop the fence. His neighbor's house is foreclosed, so no one lives there. Which reminds me, I'll be right back."

Steve disappeared and returned with three different cell phones. "We should use these."

Jenny squealed. "How cool is this? It's the first time we're using our detective phones."

On their last case, the three detectives had helped Tyrone's sister catch a robber. In the process, the thief took all three of their cell phones and destroyed them. Even though their parents replaced their phones, Tyrone insisted on giving them all pre-paid phones to use when they worked on cases.

Less than an hour later, they were making their way from where the bus dropped them off in Sommersby to Nurse Karl's house. Once they turned onto his street, they finalized their plans.

Steve glanced at his watch. "Okay, first we'll all three walk up to the door and knock. If no one answers, I'll walk to the side and peek in the bedroom window. If the coast is clear, Matt will cross the street and sit on the curb. Once he gives the go ahead, Jenny and I will use the key to get into the house."

"Once inside," Jenny picked up the story, "Steve and I will look around for anything that could be a clue and take pics of it."

"And if I see Nurse Karl coming, I'll call you guys. Make sure you've got your phones handy."

As they walked up to the front door, Steve turned to his two friends who both nodded their okay. Heart racing, Steve knocked. If Nurse Karl answered, their cover story would be that they were looking for their friend Nancy's house.

Thirty seconds later, he knocked again.

No answer.

Steve glanced around and then walked to the side of the house. The bedroom curtains were only partially open, but Steve could see enough to determine that there was no movement inside.

He joined his friends and motioned for Matt to take his position. As the tall boy crossed the street, Steve knocked one last time, just in case.

His cell lit up. All three kids had turned off their ringers to avoid making any unwanted noise. He checked Matt's text.

ALL CLEAR

After informing Jenny of the text, Steve reached into the planter to pull out the key. Within a few seconds, both he and Jenny were inside the house with the front door closed.

"Let's split up," Steve whispered.

Jenny agreed and left to explore the second bedroom. Steve moved into the first bedroom, the one they had found the music box in. No trace of the stolen museum artifacts. The room itself held very little of anything, with only the bed, a small nightstand, and a dresser.

He rummaged through the wooden dresser first, checking each drawer carefully, but found nothing out of the ordinary, just clothes. Next came the nightstand. The one drawer held nothing inside, not even a scrap of paper. Frustrated, he looked under the bed. Again, zilch. He stood slowly and sighed. Hopefully, Jenny was having better luck.

A book on the bed caught his attention. He lifted it up to see the title and an envelope fell out onto the floor. Steve reached down to pick it up and his eyes widened. It was addressed to Rosa's grandfather in Mexico. It had multiple stamps across the top and the return address came from Germany.

Pulling the letter out to read it, he frowned. The words were all Spanish. He made a mental note to learn to read the language, and then placed the letter on the bed and took several pictures of it. After taking a photograph of the return address as well, he placed the letter inside the envelope and returned it to the book, careful to lay it down in the exact same spot.

Suddenly, the ceiling creaked. Footsteps. He froze. The house apparently had an attic and someone, most likely Nurse Karl, was up there. Panicking, he reached for his phone and saw a text from Jenny:

WHAT DO WE DO

The footsteps moved and he heard a creaking door.

Steve typed: HIDE

He backed up slowly and looked around. The closet would be his best bet. He slid the door open as quietly as possible and hopped inside, sliding the door closed behind him.

He held his breath and hoped Jenny had found a good hiding spot.

Soft footsteps sounded outside the closet. Someone was in the bedroom. Steve was trapped!

6 MYSTERY MAN REVEALED

Steve's heart raced. The bed creaked. A man's voice sighed. It had to be Nurse Karl.

Biting his lip, Steve tried to come to grips with the situation. The man had just laid down. Perhaps he would fall asleep and Steve could sneak out. The soft sound of a TV sitcom filled the air. As no television set existed in the room, Nurse Karl must've accessed the channel on his cell.

Steve cringed. He could be trapped there for hours. His phone lit up and he checked the message from Jenny.

R U OK

Steve replied he was stuck in the closet.

His phone lit up again.

WINDOW N HERE OPENS. CAN U GET HERE

IL TRY

Steve thought a moment. He needed to get Nurse Karl out of the room. He sent a text to Matt, explaining the situation.

Matt replied to hold on.

A minute later, Steve heard the doorbell ring.

Grunting, the man on the bed got up and walked out of the bedroom. Steve heard the front door open and Matt's loud voice. He had to act fast.

He exited the closet, careful to close the door so the man wouldn't be suspicious. Nervous, he crept to the bedroom door and peeked out. He saw the back of Nurse Karl talking to Matt who was in the middle of some long story.

Steve leapt out of the room and into the second bedroom where Jenny stood close to an open window with a chair underneath it. She motioned for him to hurry. Steve did not waste any time. Within seconds, the two of them had scurried out of the window and jumped over the fence into yard of the foreclosed home.

Panting heavily, Steve sent Matt a quick text.

SAFE

The two kids heard Matt say in a very loud voice. "Well, thanks anyway. Have a good day."

Steve and Jenny waited a minute then joined Matt across the street and began their brisk walk to the bus stop.

Matt's face looked worried. "Are you guys okay?"

Jenny nodded. "Thanks for the rescue."

"What happened?"

With intricate detail, Steve relayed his experience inside the house, including the discovery of the letter.

"What is Nurse Karl doing with Rosa's grandfather's mail?" Jenny asked.

Steve shrugged. "I don't know, but I bet it has something to do with this case. As soon as we get home, I'll get it translated on my laptop."

Matt pointed. "Dudes, looks like the bus just pulled up. Come on."

The three kids ran to make sure they didn't miss the bus. A few minutes later, they were on their way back to Beachdale.

As the three of them settled into their seats, Steve pulled out his cell and began typing into his notes app while Jenny told her story.

"When Steve and I split up, I went into the second bedroom which was a total disaster area. Clothes were in giant piles everywhere. I mean, seriously, how hard is it to buy a laundry hamper? Or maybe, three. He could have one for dark colors, one for light colors, and one for whites. It would make the room look like a human being lived there instead of some kind of lazy slob."

"Moving on," Matt prompted.

"Anyway, I totally refused to touch any of the clothes, so gross, but I did check out the closet. It was empty. No museum artifacts, or anything else for that matter."

"Was there a dresser or a bed or anything else in the room?" Steve asked.

She shook her head. "Nope. I'm telling you, the room was totally empty, except for two chairs and the giant mounds of clothes."

Steve's cell lit up. "Hold on. Tyrone's calling." He held up the phone. "Hey, Tyrone. I'm putting you on speakerphone."

"Cool. I've got some info on that dude you were asking about. You guys wanna stop by the diner?"

"Heck, yeah!" Matt called out. "I'm starving."

"Me, too, "Jenny said.

"Make that three," Steve said.

Tyrone's laughter could be heard over the speaker. "I guess I better go make sure I've got plenty of food then."

"We'll be there in twenty minutes," Steve said.

"All right. See you then." He hung up.

"I wonder what he found out," Jenny said.

'We'll find out soon enough." Steve turned the ringer of his phone on and opened the notes app. "Anything else you noticed in the second bedroom?"

Jenny shook her head. "There was nothing to notice. Not even anything on the walls."

Her last sentence made Steve pause. He

thought back to his own investigation of the house and frowned. "Now that I think about it, there wasn't anything on the walls in his bedroom either. Or the living room. In fact, there weren't any decorations of any kind, anywhere."

Matt shrugged. "He's probably not a decorations kind of guy."

Placing the phone on his lap, Steve scrunched his forehead in thought. "I've never been in a house, any house, that didn't at least have something…a sports poster, or a mirror, or a picture frame. Anything."

Jenny leaned forward. "Hey, maybe that's not Nurse Karl's house."

In an over-dramatic fashion, Matt tossed his hands up in the air. "Great. We broke into the wrong house, and the guy I was talking to is actually an impersonator who works for the FBI and now we're going to be on America's Most Wanted, doomed to spend eternity hiding from the police."

Jenny smacked Matt on the back of the head. "Moron. I meant, maybe Karl doesn't *own* the house. He might just be renting. That might be why he never put anything up on the walls."

Steve nodded slowly. "That could also explain the lack of furniture." He paused. "In fact, I would bet that Nurse Karl started renting the house around the same time he became Rosa's grandfather's nurse."

After rubbing the back of his head, Matt put his feet up on the back of the seat in front of him. "You think Rosa's grandfather is the reason he moved here?"

Steve shrugged. "It would make sense. If his plan was to move here permanently, then he would have at least something decorating the walls, or some furniture in the house."

After pushing Matt's feet down, Jenny re-tied her hair into a braid. "If Nurse Karl only moved here when Rosa's grandfather did, then maybe he followed him here from Mexico."

The bus stop closest to the diner came into view.

"We'll pick up this conversation later," Steve said as he pulled the window cord to alert the driver to stop. "Right now, I want to hear what Tyrone has to say about Saul Mendoza."

The three kids piled out of the bus and walked the half block to the diner. The owner motioned for them to take a seat and the trio chose a table away from any of the customers.

A few minutes later, Tyrone sat in the booth next to Steve, facing Matt and Jenny.

He lowered his voice. "Okay, here's the skinny. That dude, Saul Mendoza, he's staying out at the Arabian Motel. I did some checking on him. Turns out, he was fired from that museum out in Mexico about a year ago."

Steve took out his cell to take notes. "Fired for what?"

"Suspicious activity. The museum suspected him of theft. Then, a couple days after the museum closed, he was caught on tape breaking in and stealing one of the exhibits."

Steve's fingers flew over the keypad. "Do you know what he stole?"

"A German footlocker from World War II. But that's not the whole story. The police took him to jail, but he got bailed out and then jumped bail. The Mexican police have been looking for him ever since."

"How long ago was that?" Matt asked.

"About six months ago."

Taking a pause from typing, Steve tilted his head up. "Around the same time Rosa's grandfather moved here."

"Do we know who paid his bail?" Jenny asked.

Tyrone shook his head.

"Maybe it was Rosa's grandpa," Matt suggested.

Steve bit his lip in thought. "If her grandfather had paid the bail, he would've had Saul meet him here. Rosa said she hadn't seen the man in a couple years. I think it's safe to say that her grandfather wanted nothing to do with him. Especially after he got caught stealing from the museum."

"Did you find out anything else?" Jenny asked.

Tyrone shrugged. "Nope. That's it. But you all better be careful. This dude sounds like bad news." He stood and crossed his arms. "Now, what can I get the starving detectives to eat?"

Steve and Jenny both ordered chicken fingers, fries, and a soda, and Matt ordered mozzarella sticks, a bacon burger with fries, and a chocolate shake.

After their friend left to place the order, Steve scrolled through the notes on his phone. "If Saul Mendoza was a museum thief back in Mexico, I think we can bet he's the one who robbed the museum here, too. And if that's true," he paused and looked up at his friends, "then our next stop should be the Arabian Motel."

7 A NEMESIS WITH FANGS

Steve searched for the motel address on his cell phone.

Matt groaned. "Hold on a minute. Remember what Tyrone said like two seconds ago? This guy is bad news. I'm not sure if stalking him is the right course of action here."

"The stolen museum things are probably inside his hotel room," Steve said. "And don't forget, we were hired to find a music box."

"And seeing how that's the guy who stole it from Nurse Karl's house, that box is probably at the Arabian Motel," Jenny added.

Noticing the look of worry on Matt's face, Steve decided to try a different approach. "All we really need to do is find Rosa's stolen box. It shouldn't take that long at all. You and Jenny will keep a lookout. I'll get inside the room, grab it, and then leave. We'll call the police once we're gone. Anonymously. The cops will find the museum's stuff, catch the bad guy, and we'll be able to return the box to Rosa without anyone noticing."

Matt's face relaxed. "It sounds easy enough. But how are you gonna get inside the motel room? It's not like he's gonna leave the key out for us."

"We'll have to play it by ear," Steve said.

After lunch, the detectives went to Steve's house to retrieve their bikes, then rode over to the Arabian Motel. Only two cars sat in the parking lot. The kids hid their bicycles behind a group of bushes and surveyed the scene.

Steve scanned the area. "First, we need to figure out which room he's in."

"How are we gonna do that?" Matt asked.

"You'll see," he answered and opened his backpack.

Pulling out paper and a pen, he neatly scripted a note, placed it inside an envelope, wrote MR. MENDOZA on the front, and held it up for his friends to see. "I'll be right back."

He walked into the front office and saw a man in his early twenties lounging behind the counter, watching television. Steve assumed he was the front desk clerk.

The guy glanced over at Steve. "Can I help you?"

Holding up the envelope for the clerk to see, Steve nodded. "Yeah. I need to get this to one of your customers. It's for Saul Mendoza. Can you tell me what room he's in?"

The young man shook his head. "Sorry, kid. We don't give out our clients' room numbers."

Steve shrugged. "That's cool. Can you give it to him for me? Dad said it's super important that he gets it right away."

Nodding, the clerk took the note.

Steve thanked him and left to rejoin his friends across the parking lot, behind the bushes.

"Well?" Jenny said, "Did you get it?"

Steve snuck a peek around the shrubs. "Not yet. Just hold on."

A few seconds later, the door of room number twelve opened. Saul Mendoza emerged and walked over to the office.

"Oh, no," Jenny said, obviously upset. "He's here. Now what do we do?"

Steve gave a half-smile. "We wait. If I'm right, he'll be leaving soon."

The man walked out of the office and toward his motel room while opening the envelope.

Matt tilted his head to one side. "What did you write in that letter, anyway?"

Keeping his eyes on the man, Steve answered, "Something I know he won't be able to resist."

"Like what?" Jenny demanded.

71

As the man disappeared inside his room, Steve grinned. "I wrote him a note saying that I knew the secret of the music box and if he wanted to find out more, to meet me in the reference section of the library at three o'clock. I signed it 'anonymous'."

Matt looked down at his watch. "Three o'clock? That's in like twenty minutes."

Steve chuckled. "Exactly."

The trio kept their eyes on the door to room number twelve. Sure enough, a couple of minutes later, Mr. Mendoza exited the room and headed to a white, four-door sedan in the parking lot. As he drove off, Steve glanced at the time.

"Okay, I'm guessing we've got about thirty minutes to be safe. Now that we know the kind of car he drives, I want Matt to stand watch on the street to make sure he doesn't come back early. Jenny and I will search the room, grab the music box, and get out before anyone becomes suspicious."

"How are you going to get inside?" Matt asked.

Steve pointed to Jenny. "We're going to use her mad acting skills."

Matt nodded. In their first case, Jenny had used her acting abilities to sweet-talk a housekeeper into letting them in a motel room.

They split up. Matt headed toward the street, while Steve and Jenny walked to the room.

Once they reached number twelve, Jenny went

off to find someone to let them in. Within two minutes, she returned leading a young woman in uniform, carrying an arm full of towels."

"Thank you SO much," Jenny said sweetly. "Mom told us not to walk out without a key." She giggled. "But I thought *he* had a key…"

"…and I thought *she* had a key," Steve joined in.

The housekeeper laughed. "You wouldn't believe how often that happens." She opened the door. "There you go, kids."

Jenny grabbed the towels out of her hands, "Thank you, again."

The woman smiled and left.

After placing the DO NOT DISTURB sign on the doorknob, Jenny and Steve walked inside and closed the door quickly. They shut the curtains and scanned the interior of the room. No suitcase. No museum artifacts. Nothing at all besides the motel furniture.

Steve moved deeper into the room. "This is odd."

Jenny opened the small closet. "Here's his suitcase. But I don't see the music box."

"Look inside it."

Jenny pulled the suitcase out, laid it on the floor, and unzipped it. She rummaged through the contents. "Nothing but clothes and toiletries."

Steve lifted the comforter and checked under

the bed. Nothing. The drawer of the nightstand also held nothing except the motel Bible. Frustrated, he moved into the small bathroom. It was empty as well.

He walked out and found Jenny standing with her arms crossed.

"Now what?" she asked.

"We leave. There's nothing here."

After returning the curtains to their original position, the two kids removed the DO NOT DISTURB sign, walked out the door, and crossed the parking lot. Jenny texted Matt and told him to meet them at their bikes.

"What happened?" he asked as he joined them.

Steve sighed. "There was nothing there. Not even the music box."

Matt picked up his bicycle. "So, now what do we do?"

Steve shook his head. "I don't know. I really thought the music box would be there. And the museum stuff."

After lifting his kickstand with his foot, Matt swung his leg over and sat on his bike. "That means the dude's got everything stashed somewhere else. But where?"

No one answered.

Deciding to break for the day, the kids split up agreeing to regroup in the morning.

Steve rode home depressed. He thought for

sure they were going to return the music box to Rosa today, and then use it to solve the secret of the missing gold.

He dropped his bike next to his front door and stomped down the hallway. For the first time since becoming a detective, he had no idea what to do. He swooped his laptop off his desk and plopped down on the bed, frustrated.

Plugging his cell into his laptop, he hit close when the usual NOT ENOUGH STORAGE window popped up. He jumped up. Storage! That was it! Of course, Mendoza wouldn't keep the stolen museum things in his motel room where they could be seen. He'd keep them somewhere nobody except himself would be able to get to…like a storage unit.

He typed a search for storage facilities in Beachdale. There were fifteen total, way too many for them to stake out. There had to be a way to narrow it down. He bit his lip in thought, then a slow smile crossed his face.

Steve opened the door and let Jenny in.

"What was so urgent that we had to meet right now?" Jenny asked.

"Because," Matt called out from the couch, "Steve wants us to go on a wild goose chase."

Steve and Jenny joined Matt in the living room.

"I figured out where the stolen artifacts are."

Jenny's eyes widened. "Where?"

"The one place where no one would ever find them," Steve answered. "A storage facility."

The girl clapped her hands. "Brilliant! Now all we have to do is figure out which one."

Steve grinned. "Done."

A look of surprise covered Jenny's face. "What? How?"

Trying to keep his excitement under control, Steve recounted his story. "I started calling all the storage places in town, one by one, telling them I was a student doing a project for school on people who move here from other countries and all the expenses they have. The fifth place I called said that they had a Mexican guy rent a place just yesterday."

Jenny nodded. "That is totally our guy."

Steve agreed. "Right. So, here's my plan—"

"Crazy plan," Matt interrupted.

Steve ignored him. "We go to the storage place and stake it out. They don't close until eight. Hopefully, Mr. Mendoza will either be there, or go there before they close. That way, we'll know which unit is his and we can figure out a way to get in."

Jenny's smile turned into a frown. "Hold on. Won't they have security?"

Matt leaned back. "Like I said, crazy."

Grabbing his backpack off the coffee table, Steve continued. "Chances are, all they have is a security guard. Once we figure out which storage unit the artifacts are in, Jenny will distract the guard by interviewing him for her summer school paper, and Matt and I will get into the unit and get the music box."

After putting her cell phone on the coffee table and picking up her detective phone, Jenny put the pre-paid cell in her pocket. "Just one more question before we go. I'm sure that Mendoza guy put a lock on his unit. How're you planning on breaking in?"

Steve held up a paper clip and smiled. "I've been trying this out on locks around the house. It works on most of them. Okay, you guys ready?"

"Ready," Jenny said, sounding enthusiastic.

Matt stood and stretched. "Not really. But I'm guessing I don't have a choice."

Jenny threw his backpack at him. "No, you don't."

Sighing, he put it on. "Can you at least promise me we'll have dinner afterward? I'm starving."

Steve opened the front door. "I promise. I'll even buy you an extra dessert."

Matt's face broke into a huge smile. "Now you're talking."

They reached their destination in twenty minutes. Storage For Less turned out to be a huge facility, almost a block long, with rows of storage units that cars could drive between. A guard gate meant the kids wouldn't be allowed inside, so they split up and rode their bikes around the fence, checking down every row for the white, four-door sedan. In fifteen minutes, they regrouped in front.

"He's not here," Jenny said.

Pointing to a cluster of shrubs near the front entrance, Steve motioned for his friends to follow him. "That's a good place for our stakeout. If he drives in, we'll see him."

With their bikes on the ground close by, they crouched behind the bushes and waited.

After an hour, Matt started fidgeting. He had already eaten two granola bars from his backpack. "How much longer?"

Steve glanced at his watch. "The place closes in twenty minutes. If he doesn't show, we'll leave."

At five minutes to eight, a white car approached the entrance gate. As the guard walked up to the driver, Jenny grabbed Matt's arm. "That's him! He showed up."

"Split up again," Steve ordered. "We've got to see which unit is his. And judging by the time, he's not going to be here long."

They split up, with Matt and Jenny heading left and Steve heading right. Soon, Matt stopped his bike and motioned for Jenny to join him. He pointed. "There he is. Third aisle from the back, sixth unit from the end."

Jenny whipped out her cell and made a note of it, while Matt kept his eyes on the man. From what Matt could see, he opened a lock, lifted the metal gate, and disappeared inside. Within seconds, he exited, lowered the gate, and locked it. Then, he got in his car and drove away.

Jenny's cell lit up. "Hey, Steve," she answered.

"Any luck?"

"Yeah. We know which unit is his, and he just left."

"Okay," Steve said. "I'm gonna ride to the front and wait for the gate guard to leave. Sit tight."

She hung up and relayed the information to Matt. The two kids sat on the dirt, waiting for their friend.

Steve hid behind the bushes near the front entrance. A few minutes later, a green SUV pulled up to the gate and a man in a security uniform exited the passenger side. Before closing the door, he said something to the driver then closed the door. The SUV drove away.

Steve's heart sank. If they had nighttime security, then the kids could run the risk of getting caught.

The two guards held a quick conversation before the day guy walked over to a parked car, got in, and drove away. The new security officer settled into the chair inside the booth.

Steve thought furiously. If the man remained in the booth, it wouldn't be a problem. But if he decided to patrol, they'd be in trouble.

After dialing Jenny's number, he quickly explained the situation to her. "We need to work fast. I'll stay here and keep an eye on the security guard. You two have to get the music box on your own. Do you have a paper clip?"

"Yep. I always carry one in my pocket."

Steve nodded even though she couldn't see him. "Good. You're going to have to pick that lock. Think you guys will be okay hopping the fence?"

"Yeah, it's a regular chain-link fence. No problem."

"Be careful and be quick. Just grab the music box, take a picture of the museum stuff so we can send it to the police, and get out."

"Will do."

Steve hung up and bit his lip. He had a bad feeling about this. But as long as he kept his eye on the guard, everything should be all right.

After glancing around nervously, Matt took a deep breath and followed Jenny over the fence. They ran to the storage unit and pulled on the lock. It had definitely been locked tight.

Jenny whipped the paperclip out of her front pocket. "I sure hope this works." She unbent the clip and put one end into the key hole. The paperclip trick had worked for them in previous cases.

Matt was just about to wish her luck when a strange sound interrupted his thought. He turned around slowly and saw his worst nightmare—a Doberman Pinscher, teeth exposed, staring at him, growling.

"J—J—Jenn," he sputtered in a voice barely above a whisper. "Get up real slow."

Jenny stood and grabbed the back of Matt's hoodie. "What are we gonna do?" she whispered.

"Back away slowly, toward the fence."

The two friends began moving away from the fierce hound, who followed them vigilantly. They had made it about ten feet when another sound filled the air—a second Doberman, on the other side of them, growling viciously. They looked at each other, then at the dogs. They were surrounded.

8 RETURN TO THE ARABIAN MOTEL

"What are we gonna do?" Jenny asked again, her voice trembling.

"Matt! Jenny! Hold on!" A voice sounded from her left. She turned and saw Steve, his fingers gripping the chain-link fence.

The dogs stopped growling for a moment, distracted by the new sound. Then, apparently deciding the newcomer did not pose a threat, they resumed their attention to Matt and Jenny, snarling as before.

"Are you guys all right?" Steve sounded worried.

"Seriously?" Jenny asked.

Matt gave a short laugh. "We'd be a whole lot better if we were on the other side of that fence with you."

"I have a plan," Steve said.

"You have no idea how happy I am to hear you say that," Jenny said.

"Here's the deal. You guys are about forty feet from where I am right now," Steve said. "I'm going to move down about thirty feet and climb over."

Matt's eyes widened. "Are you crazy? Then the dogs will come after you."

Steve gave a short nod. "Exactly. Once the Dobermans begin chasing me, the two of you will make a break for the fence as fast as you can. Then, when the dogs get close enough to me, I'll hurry up and climb back over. By that time, you guys will already be at the fence and should be able to hop over it before the dogs have time to double-back and reach you."

Matt shook his head. "I don't like it. What if the dogs are too fast for you?"

Steve tossed his hands up. "Then I'll just have to be faster. Look, we don't have much time. The night guard had his ear buds in, but if he notices the dogs barking, he'll come check things out. Get ready. Here I go."

"Be careful," Jenny called out.

Steve walked away from his friends about thirty feet, took a deep breath, and began his climb.

Immediately, the dogs' ears shot back and they began whining.

Steve jumped down into the property and began

rattling the fence. "Over here!" He yelled. "Come on, boys!"

Seeming to forget their current prey, the Dobermans ran toward Steve.

Matt and Jenny lost no time. The moment the dogs left their sides, they made a mad dash for freedom. Reaching the chain-link fence, they jumped as high as they could to get a good start. One of the dogs noticed and ran toward the duo, but he was too late. By the time he reached them, Matt and Jenny were already at the top preparing to jump down to the other side.

Steve waited for the remaining dog to get close, then leaped onto the fence. But not being quite as athletic as Matt or Jenny, he didn't land high enough. The Doberman jumped and caught the bottom of Steve's jeans in his mouth, trying to pull the boy down. Steve shouted, shook the dog off, and scrambled over the top.

Panting on the ground, Steve turned and stared at his nemesis, who glared back, growling, a piece of dark blue denim dangling from his mouth.

Matt and Jenny rushed up and helped Steve off the ground.

"Are you all right?" Jenny asked as she wiped some dust off his shirt.

Matt pointed at the dog. "Dude, are those your jeans in his mouth?"

Steve sighed and looked down at the torn

bottom of his left pant leg. "My mom is going to kill me."

Off in the distance, the sound of someone whistling filled the air. The two dogs turned their heads and began running toward the front of the property.

"That's probably the guard," Steve commented. "Let's get out of here."

Matt slapped Steve on the back as they began the walk toward their bikes. "You totally saved our lives, dude. We owe you big time."

Jenny nodded. "No doubt. Those dogs were going to eat us alive."

"Speaking of eating," Matt said and rubbed his stomach, "if I don't get some food in my belly fast, I may die of starvation."

Jenny laughed as they rounded the corner and headed toward the bushes concealing their bicycles. "Yeah, I'm pretty sure starvation is the last thing on earth you will die from. Tornado strike, maybe. Mobsters burying you in a concrete tub, possibly. But starvation? Not a chance."

"Ha ha. Very funny. But seriously. Can we go eat now?"

Lifting the kickstand of his bike, Steve turned to his friends. "Tyrone's?"

Matt's face broke into a grin. "You read my mind."

Tyrone had taken the evening off, so the trio took a seat at a booth and gave their order to one of the waitresses.

Closing his eyes, Matt let his head rest against the top of the seat. "Man, I am so tired. After dinner, I'm going home and sleeping for a year straight."

Jenny yawned. "Right? I think I'm gonna write my alarm clock a Dear John letter and sleep till next spring."

Steve sat up abruptly. "Letter." He whipped out his cell phone. "I totally forgot about it."

Stretching his arms above his head, Matt opened his eyes. "About what?"

After opening his camera roll, Steve scrolled through his pictures. "The letter I took a picture of at Nurse Karl's house. I meant to translate it when I got home but completely forgot."

Jenny placed her elbows on the table and leaned her head on her left hand. "Do it now."

It took Steve a few minutes to copy the entire letter into Google Translate. By the time he finished, the waitress had brought their food and beverages.

Steve took a sip from his soda. "Okay, here's what it says:

Dear Juan,

It was good to hear from you. If you are reading this, then the last of our friends is safe. I wish we could one day reunite, but my health fails me.

Enjoy life. Make their loss your joy.

Sincerely,

Erik

Once he poured a puddle of ketchup next to his French fries, Matt replaced the lid and slid the bottle to the middle of the table. "That's it? That's the letter Nurse Karl stole from Rosa's grandfather?"

Jenny pulled the pickles out of her burger and put them on Matt's plate. "I wonder who Erik is."

Steve shrugged and typed into his phone. "I don't know, but I just texted Rosa asking her if she knew any of her grandfather's friends with that name."

After stuffing both Jenny and Steve's pickles into his cheeseburger, Matt took a bite, sending one of the pickle slices flying onto his lap. He grabbed a napkin to wipe the ketchup residue and pickle off his jeans. "Do you think we should tell Rosa what's going on? I mean, maybe she should know the museum robbery is related to her music box."

Steve swallowed his mouthful of food. "I suggest we hold off on that. It could scare her."

Pushing the ketchup bottle out of her way, Jenny reached across the table for the salt shaker. "Do you think she's in danger?"

Steve shook his head. "No, especially since she doesn't have the music box anymore. Which brings up a different question. What should we do once we get the box? If we give it back to Rosa, it could put her and her father in danger again."

Matt pounded his straw out of the wrapper, then blew the wrapper at Jenny. "But what would *we* do with it? I mean, the whole reason we're hunting for it is to give it back to her."

Steve nodded slowly, swirling the ketchup on his plate around with a fry. "Yes, and we will give it back to her. It's just…"

"You want to solve the secret of the missing gold, don't you?" Jenny said.

Dropping the fry on his plate, Steve looked excited. "Wouldn't that be amazing? The gold has been missing for over seventy years. And somehow, that music box is the clue to figuring out where it is."

Jenny put her fork down and bit her lip. "Yeah, it'd be way cool to solve the mystery. But, Steve, the music box is hers. She has a right to know what we're doing."

Steve sighed and nodded "You're right. And she is our client. We should tell her everything, even if it means she pulls us off the case."

Pushing his dirty napkins to the side, Matt frowned. "Why would she pull us off the case?"

Steve unlocked his phone and began typing. "Because, she may feel this box isn't worth us risking our lives."

Jenny churned the straw around in her soda. "Or, she may be just as curious as we are to find out what happened to the missing gold."

Steve's phone beeped. He checked the message. "Rosa agreed to meet with us tomorrow. Is ten o'clock a good time for both of you?"

They nodded.

His fingers flew over the on-screen keypad. "Then it's settled. Tomorrow we talk with our client about the fate of our investigation."

Steve lay on his bed, staring at the ceiling. The clock read ten-fifteen. Tomorrow, the Decoders stood the chance of being taken off their case. It would be the first time they didn't solve a mystery. But Rosa was their client, and the music box rightfully belonged to her.

And if she did allow them to continue the investigation, then they faced a different problem— how to get inside the storage unit. Although the paperclip method could work, it would take time. When he practiced it on his bicycle lock, his quickest time had been twenty minutes, and twenty minutes with two Dobermans was way too long.

If only they had the key, then they could unlock the unit, get inside, and close the door before the dogs even realized anything had happened. But they couldn't exactly ask the only man who had the key to just hand it over to them.

An idea began to form in his mind. He crept to the hallway and peered out. His parents had gone to sleep. Closing the door to his room, he stared at the clock. It may've been too late to call Matt and Jenny, but it was not too late for him to do something.

Grabbing his backpack, he climbed through his window and quietly rolled his bike out of the driveway. As he pedaled down the street, he contemplated his plan. It was a long-shot, but it could be possible that Mendoza had left the key to the storage unit inside his car.

He stopped across the street from the Arabian Motel and surveyed the area. There were several cars in the parking lot, including the white sedan parked right in front of room number twelve. He hid his bike behind bushes and checked the area again. Nobody in sight.

The curtains were closed and no light from inside could be seen. Hopefully, Saul Mendoza had fallen asleep. This was Steve's chance. He walked to the white sedan, glanced around, and gently pulled on the passenger-side handle. To his surprise, the door opened. He climbed in, crouched on the floor, and closed the door quietly behind him.

Losing no time, he began his search by feeling around the passenger seat in front of him. Nothing. He checked the glove compartment, the cup holders, and everywhere else he could think of. No key. He sighed and reached over to open the door when he noticed a small storage place just below the handle, too small for a cup but large enough to hold loose change.

He slid his finger inside and felt around. Empty. His attention moved to the driver's door. Stretching over, but careful to stay out of view, Steve reached his hand inside. He felt something round, probably a quarter, then his index finger touched something small and skinny. He lifted it out. It was a key.

Steve used the light of his cell phone to get a better look. He turned the silver key over and saw the word *Master* engraved on it. *Master* was the brand-name of the padlock he had for his bike. This had to be the key to the storage unit.

He returned his cell back to his pocket, placed the key inside the zipper of his backpack, and carefully opened the passenger-side door. After retrieving his bicycle, Steve pedaled as fast as he could toward Main Street.

He entered the 24-hour Wal-Mart at eleven o'clock and strolled casually to the Sports department. Within seconds, a college-aged employee walked up.

"Can I help you?"

Steve pulled out the key from his backpack. "Yeah, I need to make a copy of this before I lose it, again."

The teenager gave it a quick look and nodded. "Give me about five minutes."

Steve walked around the nearby aisles, glancing at merchandise. The quicker he got that key back into the car, the safer he'd feel. What if the Mexican man decided to go out for a late night snack and noticed the missing key?

True to his word, the college kid waved Steve over in five minutes.

After paying for his purchase, he thanked the employee and hurriedly left the store. As he neared the Arabian Motel, he slowed his bike down. Everything appeared normal. No police cars or crowds of people in the parking lot.

Steve hid his bicycle behind the same bushes as earlier. After double-checking that the curtains were still closed and no random people roamed the parking lot, he made his way to the white sedan. He opened the driver's side door as quietly as he could, slid the key back into its original spot, and closed the door.

He sped home. Turning onto his street, his heart began racing. He still wasn't out of danger. If his parents had noticed his disappearance, he would be grounded for the rest of his life.

Hopping off his bike without making a sound, he wheeled it into the driveway and placed it in its usual spot, then crept to the side of the house and climbed into his bedroom through the window.

He strained his ears. Complete silence. Steve exhaled a breath of relief as he pulled the key out of his pocket. His eyes gleamed. Now they had what they needed to solve this mystery.

9 THE SILVER MENORAH

"You did WHAT?" Matt's concerned voice bellowed as their bicycles skidded to a stop in front of Rosa's house. "Are you insane? You're getting as bad as Jenny."

Hopping off her bike, Jenny shook her head. "Even *I'm* not that crazy. With no lookouts, you could've been caught. You should've called us."

Steve smiled at their concern. "Okay, next time I decide to sneak into a robber's car and steal his key, I'll call."

Matt rang the doorbell. "Next time?"

After greeting the trio with a large smile, Rosa led them to the living room where Steve and Matt sat on the sofa, and the girls on the loveseat. She offered them peanuts from a bowl and bottles of water. "You wish to know about Grandfather's friend Erik, yes?

Steve pulled out his cell. "Yes. Were they good friends?"

Rosa nodded. "Very good friends. They met many years ago at a conference in Germany. Erik worked for a large museum in Berlin. He was the one who would send those wonderful World War II artifacts to Grandfather's museum in Mexico." She leaned back in her seat, a curious look on her face. "Is there something else? Your text last night sounded important, like you needed to speak with me right away."

The three detectives glanced at each other.

Steve took a deep breath. "Rosa, we have a lot to tell you."

With many interjections from both Matt and Jenny, Steve relayed everything that had happened from the moment they accepted the case to his adventure last night at the motel.

The girl sat wide-eyed, listening.

When finished, Steve pulled up the letter on his cell and handed it to her. "This is the picture I took of the letter in Nurse Karl's house."

Rosa skimmed it and nodded. "Yes, that is from Erik. Grandfather received many letters from him when we lived in Mexico." She handed him back his cell.

Jenny placed her bottle of water down on a coaster on the coffee table. "Did your grandpa still get mail from him once he moved here?"

She shook her head. "No. Soon after my father and I moved to the United States, Grandfather called and said his friend Erik had died. That letter," she paused and pointed to Steve's cell, "was probably the last one he sent."

After taking a swig of water, Matt reached for more peanuts. "What did he mean by *the last of our friends is safe*? What friends?"

Rosa shrugged. "I don't know."

"What do you think, Steve?" Jenny asked.

He thought for a moment. "It's possible that he meant the World War II artifacts he sent to the museum. I assume it would be worrying shipping important things like that from so far away. You'd want to know if they made it there safely."

"Wouldn't he just call and ask?" Matt said. "I mean, who sends mail anymore?"

"Old people," Jenny said. "My grandma still sends me a letter every month. I think it's sweet."

Matt grunted. "You're lucky. My Nana insists on FaceTime, every Friday. Every. Single. Friday."

Rosa appeared a little sad. "You should enjoy the time you have with her. One day, it will be lost."

Matt held up his hands. "Don't get me wrong, I love talking to Nana. It's just that every week she asks me if there's any new girls in my life." His face turned bright red the moment he said it.

Steve glanced at Jenny and saw the twinkle in her eye.

"Back to the story," Steve said quickly, hoping to intervene before it got ugly. "Rosa, how does Saul fit into this whole thing? Why do you think he stole the music box?"

She frowned. "If the box is the clue to missing gold as you think, then he must want to find the gold himself."

After a few seconds, Steve cleared his throat. "Which brings me to my next question: is it okay with you if we continue with our investigation?"

Rosa sat in silence for a moment. "If the music box is the reason the robbers broke into my house, and you find it and return it to me, then they may rob us again."

Steve nodded slowly. "That is a total possibility. Which is why we'd understand if you don't want us to work on the case anymore."

Playing with the ring on her finger, the Mexican girl looked conflicted. "You have already gone through so much; is this even something you are still interested in doing? I would not want you to do something you no longer wish to do."

Steve leaned forward. "Rosa, we definitely want to continue working on this case. We'd like to not only get the box back to you, but also figure out what happened to the missing gold. But we'll only do it if it's okay with you."

Rosa smiled. "I am glad to hear that. I, too, wish to know what happened to the gold. But," she paused and frowned, "I am worried for my father. What if you return the box and the robbers come back?"

Thrumming his fingers on his knee, Steve came up with an idea. "How about this? What if *we* keep the box until the mystery of the missing gold is solved. Since it won't be at your house, the robbers would have no reason to come back. We'll keep it at my house."

Immediately, Rosa shook her head. "No. Then you will be in danger."

Steve tilted his head to one side. "Actually, I won't. Neither Nurse Karl nor Saul have ever seen me. They don't even know I exist."

Jenny's face lit up. "That's right. And once we've solved the case, we can give you back the box."

Matt held up his index finger and wiggled it at the girl. "But this only works if you don't tell your dad about us. If he finds out, he'll probably call our parents, and then we'll all be in trouble and grounded till we're fifty. Then we won't be able to see you anymore." His eyes widened and he cleared his throat. "I mean, we won't be able to work on the case anymore."

Jenny smirked. "And that would be an awful shame. You know, not being able to work the case."

Time for another intervention. Steve stood. "So, it's okay for us to continue?"

Rosa smiled at Matt. "Yes. I would like that very much."

Steve gave Jenny a gentle shove toward the front door before she embarrassed Matt. "We'll text you when we find anything out."

Rosa followed them to the front door. "Thank you."

Once outside, Jenny scooted up to Matt and elbowed him. "So, I guess we have more time for you to get the guts to ask her out."

"What?" Matt said, obviously uncomfortable with her comment.

Jenny rolled her eyes and tossed her hands up high. "Oh, come on! You and Rosa totally have some chemistry going. You *have* to ask her out."

Steve's phone beeped. He checked the text. "Let's put Matt's love life on hold for now. Alysha said she found something and wants us to come over."

Jenny picked her bike up off the ground. "We are so not done talking about this."

They reached Alysha's house in fifteen minutes. After being escorted into the study by her mom, the trio sat on the sofa facing their friend.

Alysha rolled her wheelchair closer. "Thanks for coming."

"No problemo," Matt said as he reached into the candy dish and pulled out a peanut butter cup. "What's going on?"

"I did some more digging on the missing gold. It turns out that before General Schultz, the officer who owned the music box and helped smuggle the gold out of Germany, was killed, he made out a will, leaving all of his possessions to his son, Alex. But Alex died in a car accident before he turned eighteen."

Jenny frowned. "That's so sad. He was too young."

Alysha nodded. "Agreed. But that means he died before he could get all of his dad's possessions, including the gold from the Swiss bank account."

Steve leaned forward. "So then, what happened to the gold?"

After taking a sip from her water bottle, Alysha shrugged. "Nobody knows, remember? It's a mystery. However," she paused and a smile spread across her face, "something interesting happened around fifteen years ago."

Matt reached for another chocolate. "What happened fifteen years ago?"

"One of the gold bars turned up at an auction. Someone in the audience commented on the Nazi swastika engraved on it. When they did an investigation, they discovered it was one of the missing bars from the Swiss bank."

Waving his hands in front of him in a 'hold on' gesture, Matt swallowed his mouthful of chocolate. "So, let me get this straight. These gold bars that had been missing for like fifty years just randomly turned up fifteen years ago at an auction?"

"Who put it up for auction?" Steve asked.

Alysha took another drink of water. "Here's where the plot thickens. The guy who put it up for auction received the gold bar in the mail as payment for something on eBay."

"Then the feds can trace it, right?" Jenny said. "There had to be a mailing address to ship whatever had been purchased."

Leaning back in her chair, Alysha smiled. "Oh, there was a mailing address all right. It was in Berlin, Germany, to the German equivalent of a PO Box."

Steve frowned. "But couldn't they still trace whoever owned the PO Box?"

Alysha shook her head. "When the authorities investigated, they found out it had been registered under a fake name. There was no way of knowing who sent the gold bar or how they got it in the first place."

"What did this anonymous person buy with the gold bar?" Steve asked.

"A silver Jewish menorah, over two-hundred years old, that had somehow survived Nazi Germany."

Jenny laughed. "So stolen Nazi gold was used to buy a Jewish menorah? That is like totally poetic justice."

"Poetic justice?" Matt repeated. "Isn't that an English thing?"

Jenny rolled her eyes. "Seriously, Matt, do you ever pay attention in school?"

Matt put his hand on his heart as though hurt by her question. "I pay very close attention...to the lunch bell."

They all laughed.

"Back to the missing gold," Steve said, "if one bar turned up, then the rest of it is out there somewhere. But where? Who has it?"

"And," Jenny said dramatically, "what does the music box have to do with it?"

"Alysha?" A voice called from the hallway.

"Yeah, Mom?"

"It's time to go."

"Okay," she called out. "Be right there." Alysha turned to her friends. "I have to go now. Keep me posted?"

"You bet," Jenny said and the three kids stood.

As the Decoders left the house, Matt glanced at his watch. "I gotta get home. Mom wants me to help finish cleaning out the garage."

Steve nodded. "I have chores to do, too. Maybe we can meet up later."

"Sounds good to me," Jenny said and the trio split up, each heading home.

As Steve pulled weeds from the front yard, his mind

focused on the mystery, hoping to piece together the facts. Fifteen years ago, a missing gold bar turned up at an auction. Around the same time, the Neo-Nazis offered a reward for the stolen Nazi gold. No way could that be a coincidence. Whoever had the gold must've found out about the Nazis' offer and gotten scared, afraid people would come after him. That could be why no more of the bars had surfaced since.

But how did the music box fit into this? Rosa's grandfather said the key was inside, yet the box held nothing. What could he have meant?

Later, as Steve waited for dinner, he scrolled through his notes on his phone, trying to come up with answers. Frustrated, he turned to his camera roll and began thumbing through the pictures. He paused at the photograph of Rosa's grandpa and Saul standing in front of the World War II exhibit at the Museo de Reliquias Históricas. There was the music box.

Steve adjusted the screen to zoom in on the box, then his eye caught sight of something else. He moved the zoom a little to the left and focused on Rosa's grandfather's arms. They were crossed but his left hand had its index finger extended, as if pointing at something. Steve moved the zoom over and his eyes widened. The object he pointed to was an old silver menorah.

Steve scrolled quickly through his pictures and

brought up the one of the World War II exhibit at their local museum. He moved the zoom around, and then he saw it. Rosa's grandfather had brought the menorah here, to the museum in Beachdale.

Steve leaned back. This had to be the same menorah bought by the gold bar fifteen years ago, and most likely, what the museum robbers were after. He frowned. But if Saul was behind the robbery, he would've already known about the menorah from when he worked at the museum in Mexico. Why steal it now?

Unless, the music box alone wasn't enough to find the missing gold. Somehow, the menorah must be tied to it, too. And Rosa's grandfather knew it.

10 STEVE'S FOOLISH MISTAKE

After dinner, Steve met Matt and Jenny at an ice cream shop for dessert where he relayed his latest discovery.

Jenny sipped on her strawberry shake. "Do you think Rosa's grandfather was somehow involved with the missing gold bars?"

Swirling the whipped cream into his caramel chocolate shake, Steve scrunched his forehead. "It's a possibility. His friend Erik was the one who sent him the things for the museum in Mexico. I would bet Erik is the guy who bought the menorah with the gold bar."

Matt dug his fork into his apple pie à la mode. "If that's true, then Rosa's grandpa was friends with one pretty rich guy. I wonder if he believed in the whole 'share the wealth' idea."

Steve froze, mid-bite. He dropped his spoon on

the table and whisked out his cell phone. "Matt, you're brilliant."

Matt grinned. "Thanks. But, um, why exactly am I brilliant?"

"Yeah," Jenny echoed as she reached over and scooped a piece of Matt's pie with her spoon. "Why is he brilliant?"

Scrolling through his camera roll, Steve pulled up a picture and showed it to them. "Because of this."

Matt squinted at the screen. "The letter you found in Nurse Karl's house?"

Steve nodded and turned the screen back toward himself. "Listen to Erik's last words to Rosa's grandfather. *It was good to hear from you. If you are reading this, then the last of our friends is safe. I wish we could one day reunite, but my health fails me. Enjoy life. Make their loss your joy.*" He looked up. "That could be it."

Wiping a drop of vanilla ice cream off his chin, Matt frowned. "I still don't get it. What could be it?"

Steve put his cell back in his pocket. "What if Erik was buying artifacts like the menorah with the stolen gold and sending them to Rosa's grandfather at the museum in Mexico? It would explain his saying 'the last of our friends is safe' in the letter."

Matt pushed his empty plate forward. "Yeah, but what about the whole 'make their loss your joy' part? That sounds more like a 'have fun with the money' thing. I mean, if all they were going to do was buy stuff for the museum, then why not just donate the gold to the museum in the first place?"

"I'm with Matt on this one," Jenny said. "And if he really bought all that stuff with the gold bars, then I think people would've found out about it. And the Neo-Nazis. There would be stories all over the internet about the gold bars turning up around Europe."

Wiping the remains of whipped cream from his mouth, Steve sighed and leaned back in his seat. "You're both right. Only one of the thirty bars was ever seen, the one from fifteen years ago. Still," he paused and thrummed his fingers on his chin, "perhaps we're on the right track. What if Erik did somehow send Rosa's grandfather the gold, just in different forms?"

Matt appeared confused. "What? Like in gold coins instead?"

Steve shrugged. "I don't know. But something that would be able to get through customs and that couldn't be traced to the missing bars."

Jenny's face lit up. "Hey! Maybe, he sent whatever he was smuggling *inside* the museum artifacts. So, instead of the menorah being the valuable thing, maybe Erik put something inside the menorah, something only Rosa's grandfather would know about."

Steve leaned forward, excited. "I think you're onto something. And if you're right, then we've got to get back to that storage unit. I want to get a good look at that menorah, and the other museum things, before we call the cops."

Shaking his head, Matt held up his hands. "Whoa. Hold on there. Let me just remind you of two little things: Doberman number one, and Doberman number two."

"Don't worry. I've got a plan." Steve stood. Meet me at the storage facility in one hour."

At eight-thirty, Steve turned his bike down the street of Storage For Less. As he neared the entrance, he saw both Matt and Jenny waiting for him. He laid his bike on the ground behind the bushes. "I'm glad you guys are already here."

Opening his backpack, he pulled out several sandwich bags full of sliced beef.

Matt's face lit up. "All right! I was just telling Jenny how hungry I'm getting."

Steve handed the bags to Matt and Jenny. "The food's not for you. It's for the dogs."

"The dogs?" Matt repeated, a slight hint of disappointment in his voice.

"Yes, the dogs."

Jenny crossed her arms. "There better not be sleeping pills in the meat, 'cause I am so not okay with that."

Steve frowned and shook his head. "No way would I put drugs in it. But no dog can resist meat, especially roast beef. So, here's the plan. We'll split up. You two head around to the right, and I'll walk over to the other side, near Saul's storage unit. At exactly eight forty-five, I want you both to rattle the fence. Not too loud, we don't want the security guard to come snooping around, but loud enough to get the dogs' attention. Once you see them, start feeding them the beef, a little at a time."

"I get it," Jenny said, nodding.

"While you are doing that," Steve continued, "I'll climb the fence and use the key to get into the unit. It might take me a while to find the music box and the menorah, so take your time feeding the dogs and make sure to keep them distracted."

Matt shuffled his feet uneasily. "I don't know about this. What if we can't keep them distracted? Those dogs are trained killers."

"I'll be fine." Steve raised his arm to see the time. "I have eight thirty-seven."

Matt looked at his watch. "Check."

Steve adjusted his backpack over his shoulders. "Remember, eight forty-five." He walked quickly around the property, crouched behind bushes near his target, and waited. Within minutes, he heard the faint sound of dogs barking.

Heart pounding wildly, Steve lost no time and climbed quickly, but silently, over the fence.

He rushed to the storage unit, put the key in the lock, and turned it. Click! The lock opened. He smiled to himself as he quietly raised the door. Taking his cell phone out to use the flashlight app, he took a quick scan of the inside of the unit.

"The artifacts from the museum," he stated triumphantly. After taking a quick video of the unit number and the stolen artifacts to send to the police later, he began his search for the music box and the menorah.

Matt and Jenny had waited until the appointed time, then began rattling the fence. The dogs showed up immediately, growling.

"Nice doggies," Matt said in a soothing voice and pulled out some beef from one of the sandwich bags. "Here you go. Dinner time." He threw the meat a couple of feet inside. The dogs stared at Matt then at the meat, licking their lips.

"Go ahead," Jenny coaxed. "It's yummy." She also threw down a morsel.

The dogs needed no more persuading. They gobbled the meat and looked back at the kids, tails wagging, obviously wanting more. The two detectives did not disappoint them.

"Don't throw too much at one time," Jenny warned as she tossed down another couple of tidbits. "We need this to last as long as possible."

The two friends took turns throwing the meat,

hoping to keep the Dobermans distracted long enough for Steve to get what they came for.

Suddenly, the dogs began to bark wildly at something behind them. Matt and Jenny whirled around and found themselves staring straight into the faces of two policemen.

"What are you kids doing here?" One of the cops asked sternly, moving his powerful flashlight back and forth from Matt's face to Jenny's.

"Uh..." Matt mumbled and froze, his mouth wide open. They were caught. No way out. They were going to be hauled off to jail, forced to make license plates, and then grounded for the next fifty years.

"Don't be mad, officers," Jenny's voice cut into his thoughts. She sounded sweet, almost shy. Matt knew she was getting ready to put on an act. He shut his mouth and let Jenny do her thing.

"You see," she continued gently, "we were here the other day with our dad, and we saw the dogs. They looked so skinny, and we had so much food left over from dinner." Her voice started getting shaky, as though she were about to start crying. "We didn't think it would hurt anybody if we just brought them some leftovers."

The tall blond policeman flashed his light to the dogs, who began barking wildly again. Fortunately for Jenny, the dogs were on the slender side.

"Just because you think someone's dogs are too

112

skinny doesn't give you the right to feed them." The policeman's voice seemed slightly less stern.

"We're really sorry, officers," Jenny pleaded. "We won't do it again."

"Where's your friend?" The other cop spoke for the first time. He stood several inches shorter than his partner, with dark wavy hair.

Matt just stared at him, unsure what to say.

"We saw three bikes on the ground over there," he continued. "So where's the third kid?"

"He...went...looking for more dogs," Matt muttered almost incoherently.

The officer eyed him suspiciously. "What?"

Matt cleared his throat. "We weren't sure if there were just the two dogs, so our friend went around to see if he could find any more." It was a good lie...for Matt.

"He should be back soon," Jenny added, "if you want to wait."

"I think we will," the first officer replied.

Matt and Jenny glanced at each other. Now that the dogs weren't being fed anymore, they could pick up Steve's presence and take off running across the yard. That would be really, really bad.

Within five minutes, Steve walked up. The officers shone their lights on him and the dogs resumed barking.

"Find any more?" The tall policeman questioned.

Steve stole a glance at Matt who discretely shook his head no.

"Nope," Steve replied. "No more."

"So it is just the two dogs then," Jenny said. "That's what we thought."

The shorter officer lowered his flashlight. "Listen, kids, we'll let you off with a warning this time. But no more feeding animals that don't belong to you, understand?"

"Yes, Sir," the three answered in unison.

After thanking the policemen, they headed toward their bikes.

"So, what happened?" Jenny asked once they pedaled onto the main road.

"I found both the music box and the menorah. But there's a slight problem."

"What?" Matt asked.

"They've both been taken apart. They're in pieces."

"Great." Matt said.

"Maybe I can put them back together," Jenny said.

"That's what I was thinking," Steve answered. "Since we're not too far from The Pizza Palace, let's stop there and I can show you what I found."

Matt's face broke into a huge grin. "And I can get something to eat."

Once they arrived at the restaurant, they chose a secluded table far from the front door. After Matt put in his order of a small pepperoni pizza, Steve gently dumped the contents of his backpack onto the table and spread the pieces around.

Matt whistled. "Wow. He really did a number on these."

The music box had been dissected into about ten different pieces and the menorah had its base removed and each of the candle holders separated.

Jenny lifted what had been the music box bottom and examined it closely. "I should be able to put this back together." She then picked up a side of the box and held it up close to her eyes. "It doesn't seem like it's totally destroyed."

After pushing the lemon wedge to the bottom of his glass with his straw, Matt took a sip of water. "One thing's for sure, if there was a key in there, it's gone now."

"Perhaps," Steve said.

Matt frowned. "What do you mean, 'perhaps'? The dude tore this thing apart. If anything was in it, it's totally gone."

Steve bit his lip. "That's just it. The box was already empty when Rosa's grandfather gave it to her. We're missing something."

"Yeah," Matt grumbled. "A key."

Steve stared at the fragments on the table. Somewhere here, among all these pieces, a clue lay hidden. He could feel it. He lifted the lid of the box, and turning it over, he saw Rosa's name and a date in bold black letters. This was definitely her missing music box. If nothing else, hopefully, Jenny could put it back together for her.

"We should tell the cops about the storage unit and the museum stuff," Jenny said.

Several thoughts ran through Steve's mind. "Let's hold off on that for a little bit."

"How come?" Matt asked.

"We still haven't figured out the secret of the missing gold. What if there's another clue we need inside one of the other stolen things? Once the police take it, we won't be able to get to it."

Just then, Matt's pizza arrived and he offered each of his friends a slice. As they ate, the kids decided they would wait to alert the police once they were sure they didn't need anything from the storage unit.

After Matt finished off his food, the trio each went home, agreeing to meet at Steve's house at noon. Jenny took the backpack of pieces with her, promising to work on reconstructing the music box in the morning after she helped her dad in the repair shop.

Steve reached his house, watched a little television with his parents, and then went to his room. As he laid in bed, thoughts of the music box flooded his mind. If Saul returned to the storage unit tomorrow, he would notice the missing items for sure, and would most likely believe Nurse Karl to

116

be the thief as he had been the one who stole the music box from Rosa in the first place.

Rolling over to his side, he stared at the clock on his nightstand which read 12:15. There had to be something he was missing. He could feel it. But what? Sighing, he picked up his phone and scrolled through his notes. If another clue existed, he didn't see it. He opened the camera roll and watched the video he had taken of the storage unit, showcasing all the stolen artifacts. He paused several times to study each of the individual items.

All at once, he sat up in bed, staring intently at the screen, wishing he could zoom. Unfortunately, that feature did not work on videos. One of the museum items was a black briefcase with a combination lock. It seemed familiar. He scrolled back to the photograph of Rosa's grandfather and the museum exhibit, then zoomed around the picture until he found it. The briefcase stood next to the menorah.

After staring at the screen for a few more moments, Steve put his phone down. What if her grandfather wasn't pointing at the menorah? What if he was pointing at the briefcase?

Steve jumped out of bed. He had to get the briefcase before Saul figured it out, too. As he reached over to put his clothes on, he remembered the dogs. His heart sank. No way would he be able to distract the Dobermans and get into the storage unit by himself. And it was way too late to call Matt and Jenny.

He slowly climbed back into bed and formulated a plan. The storage facility opened at eight o'clock. If he got there right when it opened, the dogs would be put away and he could climb the fence and get into the unit before Saul Mendoza had even had his first cup of coffee. Hopefully.

By seven-fifteen, Steve sat at the kitchen table, eating breakfast.

"You're up awfully early," his mom commented.

Steve slurped his cereal. "Yeah, I wanted to do some research at the library before meeting up with Matt and Jenny later."

While rinsing her coffee cup in the sink, Mrs. Kemp glanced over her shoulder at her son. "Don't forget we have dinner plans with Aunt Emily tonight at six."

Steve nodded. "I'll be here."

Just then, Mr. Kemp rushed into the room and grabbed a banana from the fruit bowl. "Good morning and good-bye. I've got an early meeting." He kissed his wife and grabbed the thermos of coffee she had prepared. "Love you both."

"Love you, too, Dad,' Steve called out as his father rushed out the door.

Mrs. Kemp glanced at the microwave clock.

"I've actually got to get going, too. I promised Mrs. Jackson I would pick up doughnuts on the way to the office." She kissed her son on the top of his head. "Love you."

Steve smiled. "Love you, too."

After finishing his cereal, he washed his bowl and brushed his teeth. By seven-thirty, he climbed onto his bike to make his way to Storage For Less. As he neared the property, he noticed a line of cars waiting outside. He hid his bike and studied the vehicles carefully. Saul's white sedan was not among them. At eight o'clock exactly, the security guard opened the front gate and the cars slowly pulled in.

Steve waited a few minutes to make sure the security guard remained at his booth, then made his way to the side of the facility. After checking that nobody could see him, he climbed the gate and hurried to the unit. He pulled out the key, opened the lock, and lifted the door. Once inside, he headed straight for the briefcase.

As he neared it, he noticed something else. Several of the items had been moved since he had been there the night before. But that was impossible. The gate had just opened. No way could Saul have beaten him there. Unless...someone else besides Saul and himself had a key. He studied the objects, trying to figure out if anything had been removed.

A sound behind him startled him. He whirled around only to find himself staring straight into the barrel of a gun.

11 NURSE KARL

The gun was pointed directly at Steve's chest. "Who are you?" Nurse Karl snarled. "What are you doing here?"

Steve had to think fast. "Mr. Mendoza sent me to get something for him. Who are *you*? Are you the one who broke in here last night?"

Knitting his eyebrows, the man looked confused. He was totally buying it. Steve decided to continue. "Did you steal the music box from here? Mr. Mendoza is gonna be real mad when he finds out. If you value your own life, I suggest you run away."

The man eyed him suspiciously. He walked closer. Steve instinctively backed up.

Nurse Karl put one arm around the boy's shoulder while keeping the gun pointed at his head. "If what you say is true, then I am going to need an insurance policy to ensure my freedom. Let's go." He gave him a shove.

Steve winced. His act backfired. He had become a hostage and nobody even knew where he was.

They walked outside and the tall man let go of Steve's shoulder. He pointed to the storage unit with his gun. "Close it."

Steve obeyed and realized he only had one shot at leaving a clue.

Matt pedaled fast up the street. It was already past twelve o'clock and Steve hated it when they were late. As he pulled up, he saw Jenny sitting on the front step, typing on her phone. He dumped his bike next to hers and walked up to the house. "What's going on?"

She shrugged. "You got me. Steve's not here. I just sent him another text."

After stretching his arms high above his head, Matt plunked down next to her. "That's weird. He did say noon, right?"

She nodded. "Yep. And he's never late."

Frowning, Matt pulled out his cell and stared at it. No new messages. "Maybe his parents needed him for something and they're running behind."

Jenny shook her head. "Both his parents work today. Besides, he would've texted if he knew he'd be late." Her voice sounded nervous.

He shuffled his feet. "Where could he be?"

Typing another text, Jenny looked worried. "Do you think he went somewhere without us?"

Matt crossed his arms. "He's done it before."

"Where could he have gone? What if he's in trouble?"

Rubbing his temples, Matt closed his eyes and thought hard. "Where would Steve go that he wouldn't need us with him and that he had to go this morning, before meeting us?"

"The storage facility." Jenny's voice cut into his thoughts.

The boy opened his eyes and frowned. "No way. He wouldn't have gone there without lookouts. What about the dogs? He would've needed a distraction."

After typing something into her cell, she checked her screen then showed it to him. "Not if he went there after eight. That's when they open. They'd put the dogs away for sure."

Matt sighed, mainly because he knew in his gut that she was right. "Come on. Let's go."

As they biked to the storage place, they tried to come up with a reason their friend didn't wait for them.

"My guess," Jenny said, "is that he thought of something last night and knew he had to get to it as soon as possible."

Matt agreed. "And knowing him, he probably

went right at eight o'clock, hoping to get there before Saul Mendoza did."

"Right. And he didn't want to call us because he knew we were both busy this morning."

They reached Storage For Less within fifteen minutes. After a quick confirmation that the security guard sat in the booth at the front, the two kids snuck around to the side. Not seeing any vehicles down the aisle, they hopped the fence and walked up to the unit. The padlock was locked. No sign of their friend.

"Steve?" Matt called out. "Are you in there?"

No response.

Jenny grabbed his arm. "Matt! Look!"

She pointed to the bottom of the unit's steel door. Someone had scratched letters into the door with a rock.

Squatting, Matt studied the letters. "It looks like it says D, a little space, then NK." He turned to his friend. "What do you think?"

Jenny nodded. "Decoders, Nurse Karl. Steve was here and Nurse Karl took him."

"Come on." Matt stood and walked toward the fence. "I guess we've got a bus to catch."

Squirming, Steve struggled in vain. Tight ropes tied him to a chair in the spare bedroom of Nurse Karl's house. Duct tape over his mouth, he couldn't even scream for help. Not that it would do any good. This side of the house faced the vacant, foreclosed lot. Even if he could scream, no one would hear him.

His only chance was for Matt and Jenny to find the clue he left and come rescue him. If they even thought to check out the storage facility, that is. He chided himself for not having sent them a text as to what he planned to do.

He glanced at the window. Although he couldn't tell the exact hour of the day, he knew his time was running out. Nurse Karl had made several phone calls in the other room. From the bits and pieces of conversation Steve could understand, the man had been trying to locate Saul Mendoza. And if he made contact, then he would know Steve had lied about knowing the Mexican man.

The bedroom door opened. Nurse Karl walked in. "Your friend, Mr. Mendoza, is a difficult man to reach. Perhaps, you could contact him for me?" He held his cell phone up toward Steve.

No way would he tell this guy about the Arabian Motel. Steve shook his head violently.

His kidnapper walked up to him and in one swift movement ripped the duct tape off his mouth.

Steve cried out. No matter what people in the movies said, that was not the same as ripping off a Band-Aid.

Nurse Karl bent down to be at Steve's eye level. "Tell me how to contact your friend."

"I don't have his number," Steve said,

truthfully. The only actual bit of truth he had told the man thus far. "He calls me when he needs something."

The man reached into Steve's pocket and pulled out the pre-paid cell. "Perhaps we can find his number here."

Steve gave a short laugh. "You can try, but that's not the phone he calls me at. I leave that one at home. This one's my personal cell. But feel free to call my friends and let them know where I'm at."

Nurse Karl scrolled through the recent numbers. Steve knew they were all to Matt and Jenny. The man let out a curse, threw Steve's phone on the ground, and grabbed the duct tape.

"Wait, no," Steve pleaded. "Please, don't put that on me again. I promise I won't scream."

Ignoring the boy, he ripped off a piece of the silver tape, placing it securely across Steve's mouth.

Once Nurse Karl left the room, Steve eyed the phone on the ground. Now that it lay close by, maybe he could get to it. He tried moving his arms to loosen them from the chair. No luck. He squirmed around to see if he could get one of his legs loose, but his abductor had tied the ropes around his legs super tight.

After fifteen minutes of struggling, Steve sighed. Impossible. He looked out the window again, noticing the sun a little lower than it had been.

His only hope was Matt and Jenny. The two of them would know that something was wrong when he didn't show up for their noon meeting. They would definitely try to find him. But what if they didn't go to the storage facility first? Their first thought would probably be Saul.

The boy closed his eyes. If they went to the Arabian Motel to search for him, they could encounter the Mexican thief. In fact, knowing Jenny, she'd want to get inside his motel room to hunt for clues.

And if Saul had been to his storage unit that morning, he would've noticed the missing music box for sure. He could be very dangerous.

Steve's pulse raced. Matt and Jenny were in trouble. He had to get out of there.

Putting all his weight into it, he tried to rock the chair forward. It moved a little. Encouraged by his minor success, Steve continued his efforts, putting all his weight forward, then backward. Finally, bam! His chair fell forward. Now he needed to push his way toward the phone.

The bedroom door opened. Steve's heart sank.

"What's going on?" he heard Nurse Karl say.

Soon the man's body moved into view as he picked up the cell phone off the ground. "Smart boy. You were going for this, weren't you?" He tossed the phone across the room into the small wastebasket near the window. "I think that is the proper place for that. But you, I think, belong just where you are. Perhaps the ants will enjoy a nice new toy to play with." He laughed loudly and left, closing the door behind him.

Lying on the floor, Steve took a look around the room to see if anything could be used to help him cut the ropes. All he could see was clothes. Then his eyes caught sight of something else. Movement, near the wall. He squinted and his eyes widened. Ants! Hundreds of them following a path along the base of the wall. Nurse Karl wasn't kidding. Steve squirmed again, trying to break loose from his restraints.

After a few minutes, he stopped. No use. His thoughts returned to Matt and Jenny. *Please hurry. I need you guys.*

Matt glanced at his wristwatch and let out a dramatic sigh. "Why is this bus taking so long?"

He and Jenny had boarded the bus toward the Sommersby house ten minutes ago.

"Calm down," Jenny said, but her face appeared worried. "We'll get there soon."

"What if it's too late? What if Nurse Karl took him somewhere else?"

Jenny touched her friend's arm gently. "We'll find him."

Matt shook his head. "I just have this crazy feeling, like we need to hurry."

Rubbing her arms, Jenny shivered, like she was cold. "I know. Me, too."

They rode the rest of the way in silence. Twenty minutes later, they hopped off at the bus stop closest to Nurse Karl's house. They raced up the cul-de-sac, then stopped across the street to come up with a plan.

"What should we do?" Matt asked.

"We need to figure out if Steve's inside. Let's split up. You go left, I'll go right."

He nodded and the two kids crossed the street to begin their investigation.

As Matt reached the left side of the house, he crouched down so he wouldn't be seen by anyone looking out. He reached the first window, which if his memory served him correctly, would be the living room. The curtains were closed making it impossible for him to see inside.

The next window had partially open curtains. Matt took a chance and peeked inside Nurse Karl's bedroom, the place where they had originally found the music box. From what the boy could see, the room was empty of people. No Nurse Karl and no Steve.

He slipped around to the back of the house and saw Jenny waving, motioning for him to join her. He raced across the backyard and met her on the other side.

"What'd you find?" he whispered.

"Steve's in the second bedroom. It looks like he's tied to a chair, laying on the ground."

"Did he see you?"

She shook her head. "He's facing the other way."

"We've got to get him out of there."

She nodded. "The great thing is the window is super old, like the ones at my grandma's house. I'm pretty sure I can open it without a problem. But did you happen to notice if Nurse Karl is home?"

Matt shook his head. "The front curtains are shut. But I have an idea. How long do you think you'll need?"

"The window shouldn't take more than a minute to open. But cutting Steve loose from those ropes may take longer. Can I get your knife?"

Reaching into his pocket, the tall boy pulled out his Swiss Army knife. "I thought you had one of these, too."

She put his knife in her pocket. "I do, but I don't have it on me. I know, note to self, always carry a pocket knife."

Matt nodded. "Okay, I'm gonna knock on the front door and hopefully get Nurse Karl talking. But you've got to hurry, okay?"

She agreed and he walked to the front of the house.

Taking a deep breath, he knocked on the door. The man was holding his friend prisoner inside the house. If he got suspicious, he could take Matt prisoner, too.

Nurse Karl answered, but kept the door mostly closed, so just his head could be seen.

Matt forced a grin. "Hey, dude, remember me from the other day?"

Straining his ears, Steve tried to hear what was going on. There had been a knock on the door and now there were voices, but he couldn't make out the conversation. A noise behind him distracted him. Someone was outside the window.

He moved his head trying to see, but the back of the chair made turning his head difficult. The window creaked, as though being opened.

"Steve." Jenny's soft voice sounded behind him. "Just hold on. I'm coming to get you."

Steve felt a wave of relief. They had found him. The knock on the door had most likely been Matt who would keep Nurse Karl distracted while Jenny rescued him.

A thud behind him meant that she had made it into the room. Seconds later, her face appeared in front of him and she removed the duct tape from his mouth.

"Are you okay?" she whispered. Her voice sounded worried.

"Yes," he whispered back. "But we've got to hurry."

Losing no time, she began cutting through the ropes. Within a minute, she had freed his arms. All that remained were his leg restraints.

The front door closed. Steve panicked. "Jenny! Hide!"

12 CAUGHT!

Steve watched Jenny slide the closet door open and jump inside, closing it behind her.

The bedroom door opened. "What in the world?" Nurse Karl's voice boomed. He picked up the cut ropes and examined them. "How did you do this?"

Steve reached into his pocket. "I...I..."

Kneeling down, Nurse Karl checked all of Steve's pockets. As he pulled out Steve's pocket knife, he laughed. "Guess I should have checked before I tied you up. You're smart, I'll give you that. But you're also a pain. No matter. Once I get the music box, I will be long gone."

"What's so important about that thing, anyway?" Steve asked. If he could get Nurse Karl talking, maybe he could pick up a clue. "It's just an old box."

After lifting the fallen chair to an upright position, he began rebinding Steve's arms. "I'm surprised your friend didn't tell you."

Steve sighed dramatically. "He never tells me anything. He thinks I'm just a dumb kid. But the way he was getting all crazy about that stupid thing, I know there's something to it. So, spill. What's up with the box?"

Nurse Karl tugged on the ropes to make sure they were secure, then sat on the floor, facing Steve. "That music box holds the secret to a missing treasure. A treasure that is rightfully mine."

Steve's eyebrows shot up. That was new. "So, if it's your treasure, then how come you don't know where it is?"

His features darkened. "It was my grandfather's gold. Someone stole it from him. But I intend to get it back."

"Whoa," Steve said, trying to sound sympathetic. "That stinks. How'd they steal it?"

The man cracked his knuckles. "By impersonating my grandfather and then simply walking out of the bank. The coward! But I figured out the identity of the scoundrel. He lived in secret, but I found him."

Trying to seem confused, Steve shrugged. "But if you found him, then how come you still don't have the gold? I mean, can't you just go to the cops and say that guy has your money?"

Nurse Karl let out a short laugh. "It is not that easy. The man, the thief, he hid the gold. And now he is dead. The only clue is in that music box. That is why I must get it back." He stood and walked to the door. Before exiting, he turned to Steve. "I will make a trade with your friend. The box for your life." He walked out and closed the door.

A few seconds later, Jenny emerged from the closet and began cutting the ropes again. "Who's your 'friend'?"

"I'll tell you later. Hurry."

Matt's face appeared through the window. He looked relieved, but didn't say anything.

Within five minutes, Jenny had cut through all the ropes. Silently, the two kids placed the chair below the window. Jenny scampered through, followed quickly by Steve, who paused only long enough to retrieve his cell from the wastebasket.

Careful not to make a lot of noise, the trio jumped the fence leading to the backyard of the foreclosed home.

Matt exhaled loudly. "Man, I thought you guys were toast."

"Come on." Steve motioned for the two of them to follow him. "We've got to get out of here and back on the bus before Nurse Karl notices I'm gone."

The three detectives took a chance and ran down the street, hoping Nurse Karl did not decide to look out his front window. In a few minutes, they made it to the bus stop.

Matt checked the posted schedule and then his watch. "We've still got like fifteen minutes."

Biting her thumbnail, Jenny glanced around. "That's bad. That'll give Nurse Karl time to find us."

Steve nodded. "We need a place to hide where we can see when the bus comes, but out of the way so nobody can see us."

Jenny pointed at the bushes. "Our usual?"

As they crouched behind the nearby shrubs, they kept their eyes open for the bus, as well as Nurse Karl.

Matt's stomach growled. "Okay, when we get back to town, I need to find food. I'm starving."

Jenny nodded. "Me, too. Lunch was like way too long ago."

Rubbing his stomach, Steve gave a short laugh. "Think you guys are hungry? The last thing I ate was a bowl of cereal at seven o'clock this morning."

Matt whistled. "You win."

Steve grinned. "I'm gonna have to pass on food, though. I've got a dinner reservation with my family. They would kill me if I didn't show."

"How about you, Jenn? You up for a bite?"

A twinkle in her eye, she smiled at her friend. "Sure. Hey, maybe we should call Rosa and see if she's free. It's been like a whole twenty-four hours since you've seen her. Aren't you going through withdrawals?"

"Shh," Steve whispered.

Jenny rolled her eyes. "I was just joking. I—"

Steve clamped one hand over her mouth and pointed with the other.

Nurse Karl ran toward the bus stop. The three kids crouched lower. He stopped, looking up and down the cross streets. He yelled something in a foreign language that sounded like a curse, then turned and walked back in the direction of his house.

"I guess he noticed you're gone," Matt commented.

"I wonder what he's gonna do now?" Jenny asked.

Steve shrugged. "I don't know."

They waited the remainder of the time in silence, keeping an extra close eye out for Nurse Karl.

When the bus arrived, they sprang from the bushes and piled inside, laying low in their seats in case their adversary still lurked around. Once the bus had traveled a few miles, they sat up.

Matt turned to lean his back against the window. "So, now that we're safe, you wanna tell us what you were doing at the storage facility this morning?"

In the seat behind them, Jenny crossed her

arms. "I can't believe you went there without telling us. Again. That's twice you've gone somewhere dangerous without telling us."

Sitting next to Matt, Steve shrunk a little in his seat as he turned sideways to face them both. "I know. You guys have every right to be mad at me. I wasn't thinking. I should've texted."

Uncrossing her arms, Jenny put her knees up and wrapped her arms around them. "Well, don't ever do that again."

Steve put his hand over his heart. "Promise."

"So," Matt prompted, "what happened?"

Steve explained his theory about the briefcase being what the grandfather pointed to in the picture, and then related his morning adventures.

After pushing his brown hair out of his eyes, Matt linked his hands behind his neck and leaned back. "You mean the music box isn't important? We've been going through all of this for nothing?"

The dark boy shook his head. "No, the music box is definitely a part of this. Remember, Rosa's grandfather said it holds the key to great fortune. But I think whatever is in that briefcase will help us understand the mystery."

"So, we need to get the briefcase," Jenny said.

Matt held up his hand. "Hold on. How do you plan on getting it? Now that Nurse Karl knows Steve has a key to the storage unit, he'll probably keep an eye on it."

"Perhaps," Steve said.

"Oh, no." Matt groaned. "I know that look in your eye. You want to go back there, don't you? You are totally out of your mind."

"We have to get that briefcase if we plan on solving this mystery," Steve insisted.

"I'm in," Jenny said. "Just tell me when and where to meet you."

"Aw, you guys." Matt sighed. "Fine. I'm in, too. But this time, I'm bringing snacks."

Steve grinned. "Good thinking."

After a bit more discussion, the trio decided to meet by the bushes near the front of the storage facility at midnight.

Although Steve enjoyed spending time with his Aunt Emily, his mind kept thinking of the mystery. What if the briefcase was gone when they got there tonight? Then what?

On the car ride home, a thought struck him. Perhaps something Rosa's grandfather kept with him at the nursing home could also be a clue. After texting back and forth, he and Rosa agreed that the Decoders would meet her tomorrow morning at nine o'clock to see all her grandfather's belongings.

At eleven forty-five, Steve pulled up to the storage facility. He was the first to arrive. Remembering the policemen from the previous evening, he decided to hide his bike in a different location in case the cops returned and noticed the bikes again. He found a large SUV parked not too far away and placed his bicycle behind it. If all went well, they would be gone from there in no more than half an hour.

When he returned to the bushes, Jenny stood there waiting. After Matt arrived, they put their bikes with Steve's and then walked around to the side of the property. Everything seemed quiet.

Steve pulled bags of meat from his backpack. "Okay, same plan as last time. In ten minutes, start rattling the fence to get the dogs' attention. I'll climb over, open the storage unit, and get the briefcase. I'll text when I'm clear, and we'll meet back at the bikes."

Matt glanced at his watch. "Check. It's five after twelve. We begin operation doggie distraction at twelve-fifteen."

"Operation doggie distraction?" Jenny repeated.

Matt grinned. "Killer name, right?"

Jenny rolled her eyes. "Let's go before I regret ever having met you."

As his friends walked away, Steve studied his watch. He had an uneasy feeling about tonight. Everything needed to go according to plan. If the policemen showed up, it could cause a problem. If the security guard decided to patrol, they could be caught.

He glanced around, nervously. Something was wrong. He could feel it.

At twelve-fifteen, he heard noise coming from the opposite side of the property. He climbed up the fence and dropped down on the other side. He walked up to the storage unit, pulled out his key, then hesitated. Everything seemed quiet. Too quiet. He took a quick look toward the other side of the property but couldn't see anything.

Deciding that he was getting paranoid, he slid the key into the lock and turned it. He pulled up the rolling metal gate and walked in.

"I had a feeling you'd be showing up here."

He whirled around and saw Nurse Karl grinning at him, gun in hand.

Steve sighed. Luckily, his friends were at the other side of the facility. At least they were safe. And when Steve didn't report back, chances were they'd know something had gone wrong and they'd figure out a way to rescue him, again.

A moment later, Matt and Jenny walked in, arms up in the air. Behind them, Saul Mendoza followed closely, gun pointed at their backs.

13 A DARING ESCAPE

Steve's heart sank as his friends moved slowly to his side and lowered their arms. With all three of them here, the chances of being rescued dropped to zero.

After intently studying each of the three kids' faces, the Mexican man smiled. "Now that we are all together, perhaps introductions are in order. I am Saul Mendoza, as I believe you already know. The man with the beard at my side is Karl Schmidt. But what I am curious about is, who are you three?" He paused, apparently waiting for them to respond.

If the men believed the trio didn't know about the briefcase or the missing Nazi gold, they may let them go. Steve cleared his throat. "We're friends of Rosa Romero. She asked us to help find her stolen music box."

Nurse Karl narrowed his eyes and glared at

them. "You are friends with Rosa? How is it I have never seen you before?"

Jenny laughed. "Seriously? Do you really think you know all of Rosa's friends? I mean, she's a sixth grade girl. Do you have any idea how many friends sixth grade girls have?"

The man's face turned a little red.

Steve continued. "We went over to hang out the other day, and she told us that her house had been robbed. While we were talking, she mentioned that one of the things stolen had been a music box her grandfather had given to her before he died. She was really upset."

Jenny took over the story. "That's when the three of us decided we had to help her. She was just so sad."

Saul pointed his gun around the inside of the unit. "How did you find this place?"

Inhaling a deep breath, Steve knew he had to make this sound good. "Total luck. One of our friends, Bobby, said he saw some foreign guy with a bunch of stuff moving into one of the units here. I mean, it's not like Beachdale gets a ton of tourists who need to rent storage space. We thought for sure it was all the things stolen from Rosa's house, so we came here and staked the place out. Then we saw you coming in and out of this unit and knew we had to get inside."

"How did you get a key?" Saul asked.

Steve pulled a paperclip out of his pocket. "No key. We used this. Trust me, when you've lost like a zillion bike lock keys in your lifetime, you learn to adapt before your mom kills you. We all carry them."

Both Matt and Jenny reached into their pockets and pulled out their paperclips.

Taking the clip out of Steve's hand, the Mexican man examined it carefully, then turned to the boy. "You children are clever. Now, tell me, what did you do with the music box?

Steve frowned. "What do you mean? We don't have it. That's why we're here. To get the box."

The two men looked at each other.

"He's lying," Nurse Karl said.

Steve shook his head earnestly. "I'm not lying. We don't have it. Why else would we be here?"

After studying the boy's face for a moment, Saul said something to the other man in German. Steve recognized the word *nein,* which meant no.

Faking confusion, Matt scratched his head. "I don't get it. If neither of you guys have it and we don't have it, then...who has it?"

Nurse Karl squeezed his lips together. He seemed upset. "Someone else must be after the box. They have taken it."

Crossing her arms, Jenny stomped her foot. "This is like *so* frustrating. Why is everyone after this thing? I mean, it's special to Rosa because her grandpa gave it to her. But why do you guys want it?"

Saul shook his head. "It does not matter."

Matt gave a short laugh. "Well, it kinda does. Seriously, dude, you've got a gun pointed at us because of a stupid music box. I think we at least deserve to know what's going on."

Nurse Karl snarled. "Tell them nothing. I have already told the dark one too much."

Nodding, the tall man agreed. "It is better for everyone the less you know."

"What should we do with them?" Nurse Karl asked.

Saul Mendoza strummed his chin with his fingers. "I think it is time the police found all of the museum's stolen artifacts. Along with the three children responsible for the heist."

Jenny rolled her eyes. "Yeah, like the cops are gonna believe that *we* robbed the museum."

As a smile spread across his face, the Mexican man slowly backed out of the storage unit. "Perhaps not. But I am certain you will have an interesting time explaining to the police what you are doing locked in this unit with all the stolen pieces. Especially, since I suspect your parents do not know you are here."

Nurse Karl exited as well, and the two men lowered the metal door. Darkness engulfed them. They were trapped.

Each of the three kids pulled out their cell phones and turned on their flashlight apps.

Matt tugged on the door but it wouldn't budge. "Okay, dudes, we've got to figure how to get out of here."

Sliding up next to him, Jenny took a chance pulling on the door. "If they call the cops, we are gonna be in so much trouble."

"There's no way the police are going to think we stole these things," Steve said.

Matt tugged on the door again. "Who cares about the cops? I'm thinking about our parents. We snuck out in the middle of the night and got caught inside a storage unit with a bunch of stolen stuff. My mom is going to flip. She'll probably bolt my window shut and put like ten different locks on my bedroom door to make sure I never see the light of day again."

Jenny made a noise that sounded like a cross between a laugh and a cry. "I guess we can kiss the Decoders good-bye."

As the seriousness of the situation sunk in, Steve took a deep breath. "Let's calm down and think about this logically. There must be another way out. Look around."

They scanned the walls and ceiling of the unit.

"Hold on," Matt said. "I think I see something." He pushed a few things over and moved toward the back. "Look up there. I think it's a grate."

Steve studied it and nodded slowly. "It makes sense that all the units would have vents to the outside to keep them from getting too hot in the summer."

Scanning the room with the light from her phone, Jenny said, "Let's find something to stand on so we can pull the cover off and get out of here."

After a few minutes of searching, they discovered a German foot locker, part of the museum's World War II exhibit. Maneuvering things around, the kids managed to finally push the locker underneath the vent. Matt, the tallest by a good three inches, stood on it and reached up with his arms. "Ugh. Still not high enough. We need to put something on top of this."

They found a large tin can like the ones sold around Christmas time filled with popcorn, except that this one felt much sturdier. Once in place, Matt climbed up and reached the grate. He held his cell up to get a better look. "I'm gonna need a screwdriver." Pulling out his Swiss Army knife, he opened the right tool.

A few minutes later, the grate cover lay on the floor of the storage unit. As the most athletic, Matt helped both Steve and Jenny up through the vent and outside to freedom. Then, just as Matt's head appeared through the opening, Steve motioned for him to stop.

"Matt, wait!"

The boy froze. "What?"

"Grab the briefcase."

Matt disappeared for a moment, then a briefcase popped through the vent.

"Catch!" Matt called out.

The case fell right into Steve's hands. Moments later, Matt joined his friends and the three of them sped toward the fence, hoping to make it before running into any bad guys or Dobermans.

Reaching their bikes without incident, they agreed to meet at Steve's home at eight o'clock, an hour before they had promised Rosa they'd be at her house. That would give them a little time to try to open the briefcase. Assuming, of course, none of their parents had noticed their disappearance and grounded them for life.

As Steve neared his house, he hopped off his bike and pushed it silently up the driveway. No inside lights on. He tip-toed to his open window and climbed through. If only he could tell his parents about the mystery. He hated keeping this part of his life a secret from them. But he knew they would never be okay with it.

A half-hour later, he glanced at the clock on his nightstand. Three-thirty and no frantic phone calls from Matt or Jenny. They had made it through another night.

After setting his alarm for seven-thirty, he rolled over and sighed. Only four hours of sleep would make concentrating on the mystery difficult tomorrow. Especially since his mind could not stop thinking about the two men at Storage For Less.

He wondered if they had really called the police about the stolen items. Then it hit him. No way would Saul have made that call. The storage unit had been rented in his name. They would've traced everything to him. Steve frowned. But then why mention calling the cops?

A strange idea popped into his head. What if the police story wasn't meant to scare the kids, but to fool Nurse Karl? Perhaps the Mexican man wanted Nurse Karl to stay away from the storage unit and all the museum stuff. And since he had been the one who rented the space, Saul must have known about the grate and that the kids would be able to escape.

Scrunching his forehead, Steve turned over to his side. But that didn't make any sense either. Why would he do that? What was he up to?

At eight o'clock, the doorbell rang. After greeting his friends, Steve led them into the living room where he had placed the briefcase on the coffee table.

Matt plopped on the couch. "Okay, so how're we gonna get this thing open, anyway?"

Shoving him over, Jenny sat next to him and picked up the case. She examined the combination lock carefully. "So, it needs a six digit combination. Any ideas?"

Steve gently pushed her so he could sit on the couch as well. "That's what we've got to figure out."

Interlocking his fingers and placing them behind his head, Matt leaned back. "Can't we just bust it open?"

Steve shook his head. "Not without knowing what's inside. We have to be careful. We don't want to break anything."

"Steve?" a voice called from the kitchen.

"Yeah, Mom?"

"Is that Matt and Jenny I hear?"

"Yeah."

Mrs. Kemp walked into the room. "Could I trouble the three of you for a few minutes? I need help moving a few things in the garage and your father's already left for work."

Matt jumped up. "Of course, Mrs. Kemp. Glad to help."

Helping Steve's mom took longer than anticipated, and once they finished, it was time for them to leave for Rosa's.

"We'll have to work on the briefcase later," Steve commented as they climbed onto their bicycles.

They reached the Romero house at nine o'clock exactly.

"My father has already left for work," the girl said as she led them into the dining room and pointed to the table. "I have put together all of Grandfather's things like you asked. There is not very much. Most of these things are what he took to the nursing home with him."

Steve studied each piece carefully. Something in there had to be a clue. The items included a razor, a toothbrush, a portable alarm clock, a small desk lamp, two pairs of reading glasses, a small stack of clothes and shoes, and a fairly large shoebox.

After examining all the other things, Steve tapped his hand on the top of the shoebox. "What's in here?"

Rosa reached over and took off the lid. "These are the letters Grandfather received from his friend Erik. When he became ill, he demanded that we bring them to him at the nursing home. He would read them over and over. They always made him happy." Her eyes swelled with tears, and she blinked several times.

Reaching over, Jenny gave her a hug.

Steve picked up a couple of the letters and glanced at the envelopes. They looked just like the one he had found in Nurse Karl's house, addressed to her grandfather, and mailed from Germany with a lot of stamps across the top. He placed them back in the box and gave everything another quick glance through. "Are you sure this is everything?"

Disappointment set in. Nothing among the man's belongings gave a clue as to what had happened to the missing gold.

Rosa nodded. "Yes, this is all."

"That is good to hear." A deep voice behind them cut in.

14 THE MISSING TREASURE

Steve whirled around to see Saul Mendoza standing there, holding a gun.

The tall man stepped closer to them. "I would not want to have to conduct another search all over town."

Stomping her foot on the ground, Jenny crossed her arms. "How in the world did you find us?"

Steve sighed and put his hands in his pocket. "I can answer that. The story he told us last night about calling the cops was a fake. He knew about the grate and that we'd be able to get out. He just made up that police lie to keep Nurse Karl from going back to Storage For Less and taking any of the stolen museum artifacts."

Matt gave a short laugh. "You mean we panicked all the way home, thinking the cops were going to chase us down, for nothing?"

Taking his hands out of his pockets, Steve rubbed his temples. "Actually, we should've been looking over our shoulders the whole time. He followed us home. And then, this morning, he followed us here."

The man smiled. "You are very perspicacious."

Matt frowned. "Dude, I think he just called you sweaty."

Steve kept his eyes on the Mexican man. "No, Matt, he said that I'm smart. But I still have a few questions. Mr. Mendoza, why steal all the artifacts from the museum if you already had the music box?"

Walking over to the dining room table, the man examined the items while keeping his gun pointed at the kids. "I thought, perhaps, an additional clue existed in another of Jose Romero's World War II artifacts. But there was nothing. The only clue is the mysterious music box. But it, too, was empty." He took a step toward Rosa. "Unless, of course, you had already taken something out."

Matt moved so he stood next to Rosa.

The girl shook her head. "No. The music box was empty when Grandfather gave it to me."

The man's brow furrowed. "That is what Karl said as well."

Stepping a little closer to his friends, Steve cleared his throat. "So, Karl Schmidt is related to the German officer that smuggled the gold bars out of Germany and hid them in the Swiss bank safety deposit boxes. That's why he came here, to this house, to steal the music box. But he didn't want the police to get suspicious, so he stole a bunch of other things, too, and then pawned them all off. I get why Nurse Karl did it. He thinks the gold is rightfully his. But what about you? Why is Saul Mendoza after the gold?"

Saul took a deep breath. "I am aware that Karl believes the gold is rightfully his, but in all truth, the gold belongs to the Schutzstaffel. And as they are no longer an entity, then the fortune rightfully belongs to the Fourth Reich."

"One question. Who, or what, is a Fourth Reich?" Matt asked.

Steve answered. "It's the Neo-Nazis' crazy idea of a new Nazi Germany."

After balling his hands into fists, Matt looked angry. "You're a Nazi? Dude, that's crazy. You're not even German. You're Mexican."

Saul smiled. "You Americans. Always so dramatic. Yes, I am a Nazi, but not the 'heil Hitler' Nazi. The modern Nazi party has a different agenda, one that gold bars would certainly help fund."

"So that's your play?" Jenny said. "You're after the missing gold to pay for some crazy Nazi program?"

Turning to face the children, the man laughed. "Again, with the dramatics. My pursuit is not much different than your American 'get rich quick' schemes your countrymen seem so fascinated by."

Steve shook his head. "With one major difference. Unlike you, most Americans are not willing to hold people hostage at the end of a gun to get what they want."

He laughed again. "Perhaps you should watch your own news programs a bit more often. But, enough of this. I want the music box."

Rosa looked confused. "But we do not have it."

The man walked toward her. "I am tired of these lies. Give me the box." He grabbed Rosa's arm.

Stepping between them, Matt pushed the man as hard as he could. "Let go of her!"

Jenny took advantage of the situation and jumped on Saul's back, her arms around his throat. In a swift motion, he threw the girl off his back.

Seconds later, Matt flung himself at him in an attempted tackle. The large Mexican staggered but did not lose his footing. He grabbed Matt by the shirt and tossed him across the room. The boy's body hit the wall, hard.

Steve moved himself in front of Rosa.

Saul pointed his gun up into the air and fired a warning shot.

The kids all froze.

"Enough! Give me the box, or I begin shooting you."

Suddenly, every door in the house opened and a swarm of police officers entered the room.

"Freeze!"

The Mexican man looked around, bewildered. In a sweeping movement, two officers had him down on the ground with his hands behind his back.

"Are you kids okay?" One of the policemen asked.

All four nodded.

Picking himself up off the floor, Matt straightened his shirt. "How did you find us?"

"Dispatch got your call. We've been listening to your conversation the whole time."

Matt, Jenny, and Rosa all turned to Steve.

Grinning, he pulled his cell phone out of his pocket. "Weren't you guys wondering why I kept asking him all those questions when we already knew the answers to most of them?"

The policeman patted Steve on the shoulder. "And getting him to confess to the museum robbery. Good job, kid."

Jenny clapped her hands. "Steve, you are so brilliant."

After SWAT hauled Saul away, a young policeman stayed and took statements from the four children. After writing everything down, he explained to the kids that, because of their age, their parents would have to be called.

Steve bit his lip in concern. If the adults learned

the details of the case, they could find out about their late night escapades. They would all be grounded for life. He cleared his throat. "Um, do you think it's possible to limit the amount of information you give our parents? We really don't want them to worry."

A twinkle in his eye, the policeman winked. "What, you don't want your parents to find out that you're the famous Decoders detectives we've been reading about in the newspaper?"

All three jaws dropped.

"You...you know?" Steve managed to get out.

The young officer laughed. "Yeah, Tyrone's a friend of mine. He keeps me informed about everything happening in town. And three twelve-year-old detectives that can outsmart the best criminals in the world is definitely something worth knowing."

Grinning at the compliment, Steve chuckled. "So, you won't tell our parents?"

The man's head teetered back and forth. "Well, I do have to tell them what happened here. But don't worry, I'll keep the Decoders out of it. Now, you three should probably head home. I'm sure your parents are going to be worried once I call them."

Just then, Rosa's father walked in and rushed up to her. "Mi niña!" He hugged her. "Are you all right?"

"Yes, Papá. My friends saved me."

As the man wiped a tear from his cheek, he turned to the trio. "How can I ever thank you?"

Steve smiled. "It was our pleasure."

"Yeah," Matt said. "Rosa is our friend."

Mr. Romero hugged each of the kids before they left for home.

Steve's mom stood waiting for him at the front door when he reached his house. She pulled him into the tightest bear hug he had ever experienced.

"Mom, I'm okay."

Sighing, she released him. "I'm so glad." Then she pulled him into another hug.

That night, Steve stared at the briefcase on his bed. The case held the secret to one of the greatest mysteries of World War II, and all he needed was a six digit number. What could it be?

All at once, he sat up and slapped himself on the forehead. "Of course!" He moved the numbers to a specific combination.

The lock clicked open.

Holding his breath, he raised the lid to the briefcase and peered inside.

Steve opened the door and greeted his fellow detectives.

Making her way into the living room, Jenny tossed a pillow to the side and sat on the couch. "I can't believe you got it open."

After grabbing a banana from the kitchen, Matt joined her. "I know. That's so totally awesome." Bending his knees, he sat down on the sofa slowly, his face expressing pain.

Steve frowned. "Are you okay?"

Matt winced. "My body is one big giant ow. That Mexican dude throwing me across the room and into the wall, yeah, it was not a happy time."

Jenny looked at him sympathetically. "We totally need to take some self-defense classes. Like tomorrow."

Nodding, Matt agreed. "Seriously. I'm there with that. But back to the briefcase, how'd you do it?"

Steve joined his friends on the couch, picking up the briefcase from the coffee table. "The secret was in the music box, just like Rosa's grandfather said."

Matt frowned. "Hold up. We checked that music box like a thousand times. Saul even tore it apart."

Running his fingers along the edge of the case, Steve grinned. "But the key *was* in the box."

Tossing her arms up in dramatic fashion, Jenny vented, "Ugh. Spill it already."

The boy laughed. "Okay. As I sat on my bed, staring at the briefcase trying to think of a six digit code, it hit me." He paused.

"And?" Matt demanded. "What was it?"

Steve pushed the combination lock so the numbers were in place. A click sounded. "The only six digit number in the music box. Think."

A few seconds later, Jenny clasped her hands together. "The date! There was a date underneath Rosa's name on the box."

Matt whistled. "That's why we couldn't find the key. It wasn't a *key* key. It was a number."

Scooting herself to the edge of the sofa, Jenny leaned forward. "So, what's inside?"

Steve shook his head and shrugged. "You are not gonna believe it."

Matt hunched forward to get a good view. "Wait. Let me guess. Stocks? Bonds? Gift cards?"

"Gift cards?" Jenny repeated.

"What? It could happen. What do you think is in there, Miss Smarty Pants?"

Jenny shrugged. "I don't know. Bank account information or safety deposit box keys."

Steve smiled broadly. "All of those are great guesses, except maybe the gift cards. But you guys are way off. Ready?"

Both kids nodded.

Anticipating their reaction, Steve threw the lid of the briefcase open and watched his friends' expressions. They did not disappoint.

Matt's eyes widened. "No…way."

Jenny's jaw dropped. "You have got to be kidding me. Steve, are you messing with us?"

He shook his head. "Nope. This is exactly what I found when I opened the briefcase last night."

Jenny just stared at it. "It's...an *iron*, right? A modern, regular, get the wrinkles out of clothes, iron?"

He nodded. His own reaction had been exactly the same. "Yep. So, I'm open to suggestions. Any idea what on earth we're supposed to do with this?"

Matt picked it up to examine. "Open up a dry cleaners? I guess that would be a way to get a great fortune."

He handed the iron over to Jenny.

Moving her fingers around the edges, she frowned. "Maybe there's a hidden compartment." A few moments later, she shook her head. "Nothing."

Steve sighed. "I texted Rosa and told her what I found inside."

After placing the iron down on the table, Jenny leaned back into the sofa. "What'd she say?"

He reached over and picked up the iron. "She was just as shocked as we were."

"An iron didn't mean anything to her?" Jenny asked.

Holding it two inches from his eyes, he examined it closely. "She doesn't even remember her grandfather ever using an iron."

Matt scratched his head. "I don't get it. How's an iron supposed to help us?"

"Maybe we were wrong about the briefcase,"

Jenny suggested. "What if this isn't part of the clue at all?"

Placing the object back on the coffee table, Steve sighed and reclined back. "But why lock an iron in a super-secure briefcase under a six digit lock and then give Rosa the combination and tell her it's the secret to great fortune if it isn't important? That doesn't make any sense. It must mean something."

Matt walked over to the wastebasket and dropped his banana peel inside. "Maybe Rosa's grandfather thought that ironing was the key to a successful life."

Jenny rolled her eyes. "Really? Ironing is the key to a successful life? Steve just said that Rosa didn't even remember her grandfather using an iron, remember? Of course," she paused, her eyes twinkling, "maybe you don't remember because he said the word *Rosa* and your mind wandered off into some sort of daydream."

Matt's face turned slightly red. "I did not."

Jenny burst out laughing. "Okay, okay. Don't get steamed. I'm just teasing."

"Steamed," Steve murmured.

"What?" Matt said.

No response.

"Steve?" Matt said.

Again, no response.

Jenny waved her hand in front of the boy's

face. "Yeah, we lost him. He's in his own little world right now."

Steve jumped up and picked up the iron. "That's it! Come on." He grabbed his backpack, put the iron inside, and then walked to the front door.

"Where are we going?" Jenny asked as she and Matt followed him out of the house.

After locking the front door behind him, Steve walked to his bike. "To Rosa's house. There's something I need to see."

"Uh, shouldn't we call and let her know we're coming?" Jenny asked.

He stopped short. "You're right." Pulling out his cell phone, he dialed her number.

"Hello?" she answered.

After a quick greeting, he asked if it would be all right for them to stop by immediately. She said it would be fine.

The three detectives rode in silence to their friend's house. Matt and Jenny knew better than to disturb Steve when he was in thinking mode.

In fifteen minutes, they were knocking on Rosa's door. She invited them in.

Steve took a peek at the dining room table. Fortunately, her grandfather's things were still on it. He smiled and pulled the iron out of his backpack. "Is it okay if I fill this with water and plug it in?"

Rosa appeared confused, but nodded her approval. Steve walked to the kitchen sink, filled the iron with water, and plugged it into the nearest outlet.

Matt walked up behind him. "Okay, now what?"

"We wait." He made his way to the dining room table. "In the meantime, I want to take a closer look at those letters."

"The letters?" Jenny repeated. "Why?"

Instead of answering, he opened the shoebox and pulled out the top one. He held it up to the light and walked back over to the kitchen.

"Do either of you have any idea what he's doing?" Matt asked as the group followed him.

Jenny shook her head. "Not a clue."

Rosa also said no.

Steve picked up the iron and pushed a button. A puff of steam billowed out. He grinned. Perfect.

While the other kids looked on, Steve held up the envelope with one hand, put the iron close to the front of it, and pushed the button.

He watched as the steam began to dampen the paper. This just had to work. Several seconds later, he put the iron down and ran his fingernail along the edges of the multiple stamps. In a few seconds, he peeled them all off. There, hidden underneath, lay a single stamp, encased in what appeared to be a miniature sheet protector. He carefully peeled it off, then dropped the envelope onto the table as he thoroughly examined his find.

Matt frowned. "What the heck? Why is there a stamp underneath all the other stamps?"

Picking up the damp envelope, Jenny shrugged. "Maybe he tried mailing it and it didn't have enough postage so he threw a bunch more stamps on top."

Steve held it up for the others to see. "This stamp is protected by a stamp mount. Philatelists use them to protect their collections."

Matt looked confused. "Philatelist? Isn't that some kind of a violin band or something?"

Steve sighed. "No, Matt, a *philharmonic* is a symphony orchestra. A *philatelist* is a person who collects stamps." He pulled out his cell and did a search online.

Jenny crossed her arms. "I still don't get it. Why would Eric be sending Rosa's grandfather his stamp collection? And why hide them underneath the other stamps?"

Steve held up his screen so the other kids could see. "This is why."

One glance at the monitor and Matt's jaw dropped. "Holy smokes! That stamp is worth thirty thousand dollars!"

15 ROSA'S UNEXPECTED THANK YOU

After a few more moments of studying the website, Steve put his phone back in his pocket, walked to the couch, and sat down. The others followed.

"Here's my theory. Erik acquired the gold bars fifteen years ago. From whom or where I don't think we'll ever really know. Because he loved World War II stuff, I think he originally wanted to use the Nazi gold to buy valuable objects. But after he paid for the silver menorah, the gold bar turned up at that auction and people around the world found out."

"Including our crazy buddy, Saul," Matt said.

"And the Neo-Nazis," Jenny added.

"So, Erik had to come up with a different idea. According to that website, this stamp had been purchased ten years ago by an anonymous buyer who paid for it using a gold bar engraved with the symbol of a black plus sign outlined with a black square."

Matt held up his hand. "Hold up. The stolen Nazi bars had swastika symbols, so this can't be the same one."

Steve leaned forward. "I'm pretty sure it is. Erik knew he couldn't get rid of the Nazi bars the way they were, so he changed the way they looked. Think about it. If you take the ends of each stem of the swastika and extend them, they form a square."

Tracing the design with her finger in the air, Jenny nodded. "You're right. It would form a square with a plus sign inside."

"Exactly. If we searched underneath the stamps of each of the letters in that shoebox, I bet we'd find other valuable stamps. I think Erik planned on getting the fortune out of Germany to your grandfather, and then joining him in Mexico. But he got sick and couldn't make the trip."

Jenny clapped her hands once. "That's it! That's why in his last letter, the one Nurse Karl had at his house, Erik wrote *I wish we could one day reunite, but my health fails me. Enjoy life. Make their loss your joy.* He knew he wouldn't be able to travel, so he wanted Rosa's grandpa to spend the money."

Steve nodded. "And that letter probably has the last of the secret stamps. That's why he wrote *if you are reading this, then the last of our friends is safe.*"

169

Matt jumped up. "Well, what are we waiting for? Let's check out those other stamps!"

Steve grabbed his arm and pulled him back onto the couch. "I don't think so."

"Why not?" Matt demanded.

"We were lucky I didn't mess up this stamp with the iron. Too much steam and I could've ruined it. The rest of them need to be removed by a professional. The museum has a sweat box. They can use it to get to all the stamps without hurting them."

Jenny stood. "Then let's take a trip to the museum."

All the kids rose except Steve.

"Steve?" Jenny asked. "Don't you want to come?"

The boy sighed. "Want to? Yes. But the museum will want to know how Rosa figured this all out."

The girl grinned. "And I will be happy to tell them how my three friends helped me discover the secret."

The smiles on both Matt and Jenny's faces disappeared. Jenny hung her head. "Now I get it." She turned to the girl. "Rosa, you can't tell them about us. Our parents can't know we're the Decoders."

After collapsing back down onto the sofa, Matt winced in pain and pushed his brown hair behind his ears. "If they ever found out *we* were the reason Saul was at your house with a gun, we'd be banned from solving mysteries for the rest of our lives. Maybe even longer."

Playing with the ring on her finger, the Mexican girl looked sad. "But then how will I explain this if I cannot tell anyone about you?"

Steve smiled. "We didn't say you couldn't tell anyone about us, you just can't use our real names. Tell your dad you hired the Decoders to solve the mystery. The only thing you will have to leave out is our real identities."

Jenny sat on the arm of the couch. "Tell him you read about the Decoders in the newspaper, which is the truth, and that you asked Alysha to contact us for you."

"Which is also true," Matt added.

Steve nodded. "If you let us use your computer, we'll print something up right now, explaining everything, and sign it the *Decoders*. That letter is what you can use, along with this stamp, to show both your father and the museum. It won't be the first time the museum has gotten a letter from us."

Walking over to the laptop on the coffee table, Rosa smiled. "I do not know how I will ever be able to thank you."

Steve bit his lip and handed the girl the stamp. "There is one way."

Her eyebrows shot up. "Yes, how?"

He hesitated. "See if you can convince your dad to let Alysha write a story about this for the newspaper. It would be great publicity for the Decoders."

Staring at the treasure in her hand, she laughed. "I do not think that will be a problem."

The four kids spent the next half-hour on the computer putting together the story of the missing gold. Satisfied the note held all the important facts while still concealing their identities, the detectives left so Rosa could call her father.

"So, what now?" Matt said as they walked to their bikes.

"I gotta help Dad in the shop for a while," Jenny said. "Maybe we can meet up later?"

The kids agreed and split up.

At five o'clock, Steve received a text from Rosa asking if the three kids could meet her and Alysha for dinner at Tyrone's.

After confirming with both Matt and Jenny, he replied, agreeing to meet them at six.

Steve walked into the diner at the appointed time and saw that he was the last to arrive. Matt moved over so his friend could sit next to him in the booth.

Alysha pushed her wheelchair close to the table. "Okay, now that Steve's here, I think you should tell all of them what happened at the museum."

Playing with the straw in her water glass, Rosa began the story. "I told my father about how I hired detectives to find Grandfather's stolen music box. He was not happy that I had involved other people. Then I explained everything you had found, including the truth about Nurse Karl and Saul Mendoza."

"Both of whom are now in jail," Alysha added.

The girl nodded. "Yes. I showed father the note you wrote and he could not believe his eyes. We took the box of letters and the stamp to the museum, like you said. The man at the desk looked at the note and immediately called the boss. The two of them led us to a room where they used a machine to steam the envelopes."

Steve leaned forward. "Did you find more hidden stamps?"

The shy girl smiled. "Yes. Many. The boss called a friend of his and found out the total value of all the stamps."

"And?" Jenny prompted.

"Three million US dollars."

Steve, Matt, and Jenny stared at her.

Alysha laughed. "Told you they'd be speechless."

Once he recovered from the shock, Steve grinned. "That's fantastic, Rosa. Now you and your dad will never have to worry about money again."

"I told my father we had to thank the Decoders

for their help. Without you, we would never have known we owned such treasure."

The three kids all shook their heads simultaneously. "The Decoders don't work for money," Steve said.

Matt put a straw in his glass of water. "That's right. We do this to help people, remember?"

The girl giggled. "I remember that is what you said when we first met. But this is different. We must thank you. That is why we have set up an account for you at the local bank. Tomorrow, we will have ten thousand dollars deposited in it for you to use for your future investigations."

Matt spit out the water in his mouth. "Ten thousand dollars?"

Steve frowned. "Rosa, that is very nice of you, but we can't accept it."

She shook her head. "It is done. My father insisted on it."

Pulling a stack of napkins from the dispenser, Jenny handed them to Matt. "I'm with Steve on this one. It's way too much money. Besides, we wouldn't even be able to take money out without letting people know we're the Decoders."

Alysha smiled slyly. "Actually, that's already been taken care of as well."

Rosa explained. "Since Tyrone is the only adult who knows the secret of the Decoders, he will be the only one who can access your account directly."

She reached into her purse and pulled out three debit cards. "But when you need money, or if you need to buy anything for your cases, you can use these." She handed each of the three kids a card.

Steve looked down at the blue card in his hand. It had his name spelled out in capital letters. He shook his head and tried to hand the card back to the girl. "It's still too much money."

Rosa crossed her arms and a frown formed on her face. "Do not argue with a Latina woman. You will not win."

A moment of silence elapsed and then everyone laughed.

Just then, Tyrone brought over a giant mound of nachos. "I figure my favorite fortune finders could use an appetizer before dinner."

Matt's eyes widened. "Greatest. Nachos. Ever!" He picked up a loaded chip and stuffed it into his mouth. The other kids followed his example.

The owner of the diner pushed Steve over so he could sit next to him. "Man, you guys have been busy these last couple days."

Steve swallowed his mouthful of food. "Tell me about it. Hey, Tyrone. Do you know of any self-defense classes offered nearby?"

Scooping some guacamole onto a tortilla chip, Matt nodded. "We seriously need some Jackie Chan moves to help us out with the bad guys."

The tall man leaned back into the seat and thrummed his fingers on his chin. "Actually, my friend down at the Y teaches some beginning martial arts classes. I'll let him know the three of you are interested."

"Thanks." Steve reached for his water glass. "And thanks for these nachos. They're amazing."

Once Tyrone left to put in their dinner orders, Rosa cleared her throat. "There is one more thing I must tell you. My father and I are leaving tomorrow for Los Angeles to meet with the man who is going to purchase the stamps. After that, we will go to Mexico. My father wants to surprise our family with the good news."

Matt wiped some salsa off his face. "They're definitely gonna flip when you tell them."

"Then," she continued and began playing with the ring on her finger again, "we will return to pack our things and we will be moving to San Diego to join my aunt."

Matt froze, a nacho half-way to his mouth. "You're moving?"

Reaching over, Jenny gave Rosa a hug. "I know I speak for all of us, some of us more than others, when I say we're really going to miss you."

She released Rosa from her grip and threw Matt a sympathetic look.

"I will miss you all as well. Very much. You are the only friends I have here in America."

Steve smiled. "And you are always welcome to come visit us whenever you want."

Jenny clapped her hands. "For sure. We're not that far from San Diego. And you can stay at my house."

"Or mine," Alysha added. "I would love to do a follow up story. Think your father would let you come out for a visit?"

She grinned broadly. "I believe my father will say yes. And," she cast a shy glance toward Matt, "I would very much like to see you all again soon."

For the next couple of hours, the group laughed as they recounted their adventures, and Steve told his story of trying to explain the dog-torn jeans to his mom.

At eight-thirty, Mr. Romero came to pick up Rosa so they could leave for Los Angeles. He waited in the car as the girl said good-bye to her friends.

"I will text you once we have deposited the money into the account."

Alysha reached up and hugged her. "I hope you text me a lot more often than that."

After hugging both Jenny and Steve, Rosa walked up to Matt. "I think that you are the nicest boy I have ever met, and I will never forget you." She reached over and gave him a big, wet kiss, causing Matt's face to turn a very bright shade of red.

Steve looked over at Jenny and grinned—Matt was so never going to live this down!

BOOKS BY ALBA ARANGO

The Decoders Series

The Magic Sapphire

The Lady Ghost

The Sleepwalking Vampire

The Mysterious Music Box

The Statue of Anubis

The Miner's Gold

The JJ Bennett: Junior Spy Series

Problems in Prague

Jeopardy in Geneva

Bedlam in Berlin

Danger in Dublin

Last Stand in London

ABOUT THE AUTHOR

Alba Arango is the author of the Decoders series as well as the JJ Bennett: Junior Spy series. She lives in Las Vegas, Nevada, where she is a retired high school teacher turned full-time author. She loves coffee and chocolate (especially together...white chocolate mocha is the best!).

To learn more about Alba, visit her website at AlbaArango.com.
Instagram @AlbaArango.007
Twitter @AlbaArango007
Facebook: Alba Arango Author Page